*THREE HANDSOME BROTHERS—
ALL OFFICERS OF THE LAW—ONE
LEGENDARY CRADLE AND THREE
POWERFUL LOVE STORIES*

LULLABIES AND LOVE, the brand-new
miniseries by *USA Today* bestselling author
Sharon De Vita.

Silhouette Romance is proud to present
book one of this new miniseries. A fabulous

selection you won't want to put down!

Praise for Sharon De Vita's previous work:

"A top-notch love story… Once again, Ms. De Vita
salutes the human spirit with richly drawn
characters, genuine dialogue, fiery passion and
rock-solid plotting."—*Romantic Times* Magazine

"This story is packed full to the brim and
overflowing with emotions…
CHILD OF MIDNIGHT will make you think and
make you feel, and leave you with a profound
feeling of peace."—*Rendezvous*

*Watch for more books in the series, coming in
1998 from this award-winning author!*

Dear Reader,

Silhouette Romance is celebrating the month of valentines with six very special love stories—and three brand-new miniseries you don't want to miss. *On Baby Patrol,* our BUNDLE OF JOY selection, by bestselling author Sharon De Vita, is book one of her wonderful series, LULLABIES AND LOVE, about a legendary cradle that brings love to three brothers who are officers of the law.

In *Granted: Big Sky Groom,* Carol Grace begins her sparkling new series, BEST-KEPT WISHES, in which three high school friends' prom-night wishes are finally about to be granted. Author Julianna Morris tells the delightful story of a handsome doctor whose life is turned topsy-turvy when he becomes the guardian of his orphaned niece in *Dr. Dad.* And in Cathleen Galitz's spirited tale, *100% Pure Cowboy,* a woman returns home from a mother-daughter bonding trip with the husband of her dreams.

Next is *Corporate Groom,* which starts Linda Varner's terrific new miniseries, THREE WEDDINGS AND A FAMILY, about long-lost relatives who find a family. And finally, in *With This Child...,* Sally Carleen tells the compelling story of a woman whose baby was switched at birth—and the single father who will do anything to keep his child.

I hope you enjoy all six of Silhouette Romance's love stories this month. And next month, in March, be sure to look for *The Princess Bride* by bestselling author Diana Palmer, which launches Silhouette Romance's new monthly promotional miniseries, VIRGIN BRIDES.

Regards,

Joan Marlow Golan
Senior Editor

Please address questions and book requests to:
Silhouette Reader Service
U.S.: 3010 Walden Ave., P.O. Box 1325, Buffalo, NY 14269
Canadian: P.O. Box 609, Fort Erie, Ont. L2A 5X3

ON BABY PATROL

Sharon De Vita

Silhouette

R O M A N C E™

Published by Silhouette Books

America's Publisher of Contemporary Romance

This book is dedicated to my editor, Cristine Grace, with my deepest appreciation for extending a helping hand and gently leading me out of that long, dark tunnel. Your confidence, your support and your endless patience mean more than I can ever say. You gave me a chance and the confidence to believe in myself again, and words cannot express my gratitude. You're one in a million. May we do a hundred more books together.

 SILHOUETTE BOOKS

ISBN 0-373-19276-2

ON BABY PATROL

Books by Sharon De Vita

Silhouette Romance

Heavenly Match #475
Lady and the Legend #498
Kane and Mabel #545
Baby Makes Three #573
Sherlock's Home #593
Italian Knights #610
Sweet Adeline #693
†*On Baby Patrol* #1276

Silhouette Special Edition

Child of Midnight #1013
*The Lone Ranger #1078
**The Lady and the Sheriff* #1103
**All It Takes Is Family* #1126

*Silver Creek County
†Lullabies and Love

SHARON DE VITA

is an award-winning author of numerous works of fiction and nonfiction. Her first novel won a national writing competition for Best Unpublished Romance Novel of 1985. This award-winning book, *Heavenly Match*, was subsequently published by Silhouette in 1986.

A frequent guest speaker and lecturer at conferences and seminars across the country, Sharon is currently an Adjunct Professor of Literature and Communications at a private college in the Midwest. With over one million copies of her novels in print, Sharon's professional credentials have earned her a place in *Who's Who in American Authors, Editors and Poets* as well as the *International Who's Who of Authors*. In 1987, Sharon was the proud recipient of the *Romantic Times* Lifetime Achievement Award for Excellence in Writing.

She currently makes her home in a small suburb of Chicago, with her two college-age daughters and her teenage son.

Dear Reader,

I wanted to share with you my absolute joy and excitement about my first Silhouette Romance title in eight years. *On Baby Patrol* is a very special book to me. It's the first of my new three-book miniseries called LULLABIES AND LOVE about the fabulous Sullivan brothers—third-generation Irish cops who are strong, proud and stubborn, yet share a profound sense of duty, responsibility and pride in their family and their heritage.

This miniseries is very close to my heart. Families and their intricate relationships have always fascinated me. And being a mother of three, children hold a very special place in my heart and are an important part of this series, as well.

I wanted to create a very special series that celebrated not just families, but the enduring power and mystery of love, and the wonderful men and women who ultimately bring and hold families together with their strength and their character.

Having grown up in an Irish family gave me a special appreciation for the cultural heritage each of us inherits from our ancestors, a heritage we pass on from one generation to another no matter what our cultural background or birthplace.

On Baby Patrol is the story of Michael, the oldest Sullivan brother. In the coming months, you'll meet Danny Sullivan and Patrick Sullivan. See how an heirloom cradle brings them love and bundles of joy. I hope you grow to love these men as much as I do.

Sharon De Vita

Prologue

Dingle Peninsula
County Kerry, Ireland

He was about to lose the only woman he'd ever loved.

Desolate, he stood atop the jagged cliffs overlooking the foaming waters of Coumeenoole Strand. Night had come quickly, like an impatient lover's arms the darkness had enveloped the barren countryside in a quick, fervent caress. The foaming whitecapped sea rolled slowly toward shore. The soft slapping sound echoed through the darkness, playing a soft, haunting melody that matched his mood.

She would never be his.

He shook his head, unable to believe such blasphemy. But t'was to be. Today at the Puck Fair her clan had pledged her to another.

In front of his shocked eyes, he'd watched as the 'Wedding Matcher' had taken her hand and given it to another, sealing her fate, and dooming his.

It had broken his heart.

Bitter, he'd thought of all the plans they'd made. Since

they were wee ones they'd known they were destined for each other. She was his other half; his soul.

He'd known it the moment he'd laid eyes on her. With her fiery red hair, dancing green eyes and lips that could make the angels sing, one glance at her and he'd lost his tender heart forever.

He knew he would never—could never love another.

He thought of all the plans they'd made in the quiet of night when they'd snuck out to these jagged cliffs and held each other tightly, whispering of their love, their future, their sons. He thought now of the life they'd craved, the dreams they'd spun, the plans they'd made. For the future; their future.

He thought of the cradle he'd carved with such care. Intricate and beautiful, it was to be a wedding gift for his love, for the strong, strapping sons she would bless him with. Sons who would carry his name and one day have sons of their own, sons who would one day fulfill their own destiny, find their own true love.

And one day have sons of their own.

The cradle was to have been a thread from one generation to another, to have been given when each had found their own true love. The cradle was to have served as a remembrance of those who had come before them, of the enormous love they'd been a part of and shared, of the memories and traditions that had been carried on by the Sullivan clan for centuries.

Alas, it was to have been his and Molly's legacy; a precious keepsake for future generations of the clan so they would always know of their endless enduring love.

Aye, now he knew it was for naught.

Impotently his fists clenched and he took a deep breath, letting it out slowly. Now, he wanted to toss the cradle into the foaming sea, to watch the smooth, fine wood crash and splinter against the rocks, the way his heart had been splintered.

She was never to be his.

No!

He shook his head. He couldn't bear the thought.

A cold, bitter drizzle began to fall, hiding his tears.

His heart ached, for he knew there would never be another love. Not for him.

Only Molly.

Watching the foaming sea, his chin lifted; pride and anger surged through him.

He was a Sullivan, one of six brothers. They were a proud, strong clan and did not take defeat lightly. They'd been taught to fight for what was rightfully theirs. To do any less would bring shame to their name and their clan. Something no Sullivan would ever allow.

He would not sit by and let his only love slip away. Nay, he couldn't, not and live with himself. There'd be no reason for living if she wasn't his.

Molly belonged to him as surely as if they'd been tethered together at birth.

He knew it and so did she.

Defeat was not a word he could live with, nay, not and live with himself. Pride, love and his aching heart refused to accept what destiny had decreed.

He could not allow her to marry another no matter what her clan dictated.

Determined now, he turned his face to the sea, letting the soft mist and the brisk wind bathe his face.

He'd been gifted with an equal amount of temper and reason. He knew he'd need both now, to think, to plan. His future—their future—depended on it, and so did the future of the Sullivan clan.

He thought of the cradle again, and determination filled him, strengthening his resolve and curling his fists.

He still had time, a chance perhaps. Molly's match was set for morn'. He still had a few hours left, and maybe just maybe…

Smiling now, he turned from the foaming sea. He knew now what he must do.

His life, their life and the destiny of the clan depended on it.

Chapter One

Joanna Grace was definitely, undeniably, unbelievably...pregnant. Almost six months pregnant. And everyone in the unusually close-knit neighborhood of Logan Square on Chicago's west side knew it.

Ever since her husband, Brian, had been killed in the line of duty four months ago, the whole neighborhood had been keeping an eye out for her, whether she wanted an eye kept out for her or not. Not that she wasn't grateful. With no family of her own, and now no husband, she enjoyed the feeling of belonging, of being accepted, of feeling part of something larger. It was a luxury she'd never experienced before, but at times she found it a bit overwhelming.

There was, Joanna had realized rather quickly, quite a difference between being helpful and being downright...nosy. And unfortunately, Mrs. O'Bannion, her landlady and a cop's widow herself, had not yet learned the difference between the two. And now Joanna just knew she was going to get caught.

Shifting a sack of groceries from one hip to the other

as she searched for her house keys, Joanna absently waved to her landlady, trying to stifle a smile. She wondered if Mrs. O'Bannion knew just how much she resembled Miss Piggy when she pressed her nose against the window like that.

"Morning, Mrs. O'Bannion," Joanna called with a nod, gritting her teeth behind a smile. From experience she knew that within twenty seconds of spotting her, Mrs. O'Bannion would be on the phone tattling to everyone in the neighborhood that poor, pregnant Joanna was once again *lugging* groceries around.

No wonder the crime rate in the neighborhood was so low, Joanna mused, as she continued to dig in the pocket of her maternity jumper in search of her elusive keys. It wasn't just the fact that the neighborhood was located a mere three blocks from the 14th District Police Station, but that muggers and burglars alike had undoubtedly heard about Mrs. O'Bannion and her nosy nose. The elderly widow was probably more of a deterrent to crime than all the cops cruising the neighborhood.

Joanna's fingers closed over her metal key ring and she sighed in relief. Hopefully she'd be able to get up the steps and into the house before Mrs. O'Bannion called for reinforcements. Not that she would ever do anything to jeopardize her baby. On the contrary, this baby meant more to her than anything in the world. It was, in fact, the only thing she *had* in the world; the only thing that had ever been truly hers. But she hardly considered a can of Squirt, a dozen eggs, a chunk of Colby cheese and a few miscellaneous toiletries a dangerous load. But she had a feeling Mrs. O'Bannion wouldn't quite see it that way.

Wistfully, Joanna glanced up the stairs, remembering when she'd gamely taken them two at a time, never giving a thought to her movements. She glanced down at herself and wrinkled her nose. Now, she could barely *see* the stairs over her growing belly, so moving at anything other than a careful snail's pace was nothing more than wishful thinking.

Shifting the bag to her other hip, Joanna grabbed the banister and slowly began climbing the steps. The brisk March wind whipped around her, tossing her long blond hair to and fro. She should have caught her hair up in a ponytail this morning in order to keep it out of her face, but she just hadn't had the patience. Right now, in her condition, patience wasn't one of her long suits, and any little thing was likely to set her off.

Like the unmarked police car nearly running aground at the curb as it screeched to a halt.

Rats! Caught again! Silently cursing Mrs. O'Bannion, Joanna thought of making a dash for it, then remembered her condition. It was going to be a few more months before she could even *think* of doing any dashing.

With a soft sigh, Joanna paused on the steps, but didn't bother to turn around. She didn't have to. Only one person she knew had the audacity to drive that way in *this* neighborhood. She held her breath waiting for the explosion she knew was coming.

"Joanna Grace, what on *earth* do you think you're doing?"

Lieutenant Michael Sullivan's deep, masculine voice thundered through the air, and Joanna couldn't help but smile. He was using his scare-the-dickens-out-of-the-bad-guys cop voice again. Too bad it didn't scare her; it merely amused her. But she didn't think it wise to point that out to him. Male pride could be a dangerous thing.

Poor Michael. She wanted to sigh in exasperation. He was such a creature of habit she didn't even have to turn around to look at him. He was no doubt standing in the middle of the sidewalk—no, with his size, he'd be *blocking* the sidewalk. Clenched fists on hips, his long legs would be planted far apart and solidly on the ground. His black leather bomber jacket was no doubt unzipped, his black hair blowing in the breeze, while his dark brows would be drawn over crystal blue eyes that had darkened to a near navy. Something they always did whenever Michael was annoyed or worried. There was probably a deep scowl on that incredible face, a face she'd always thought was far too handsome for any sane woman's peace of mind. Michael had the kind of face that immediately told a smart woman he was going to be trouble—big trouble. Experience had taught her that men who looked as good as him inevitably were.

"Hello, Michael," she said, turning her head and trying not to roll her eyes. She couldn't help it. He was standing exactly as she'd envisioned him. If any other man had spoken to her in that tone of voice, she probably would have bopped him, but this was Michael. Her late husband's partner and the man who'd become her friend and self-appointed guardian angel since the day she'd been widowed. The fact that she didn't want or need a guardian angel hadn't phased Michael one bit, which had caused more than a few moments of tension between them the past few months.

Still scowling and shaking his head, Michael's long legs ate up the stairs and he was beside her in an instant. "Joanna." He sighed in exasperation, his big hands reaching for the bag of groceries in her arm.

She stubbornly hung on, refusing to relinquish the bag, starting a virtual tug-of-war between them in the middle of the stairs. Her independence was her most valuable commodity at the moment and she clung to it tenaciously. Perhaps because at times she felt it was her *only* commodity. In her precarious condition, both physical and emotional, she hated the thought that she might unwittingly become dependent on someone. *Especially* Michael. It would have been easy because of his generous nature, but she simply couldn't allow it.

"Michael." It was her turn to sigh in exasperation; she didn't bother to hide it. She figured her condition warranted some leeway. "I've told you. I'm more than capable of going to the store, not to mention taking care of myself." There was a hint of bite to her words, making him look at her curiously. They'd been going around and around about this for the past four months.

She wasn't being rude, nor ungrateful. Merely practical. Except for her brief marriage, she'd been alone for most of her life. Being alone had taught her to be totally self-sufficient.

She'd never had the luxury of depending on anyone, and her brief marriage had only reinforced the necessity for self-reliance. Anything less merely led to pain and heartache, or worse, abandonment. She figured she'd had her fair share of all three.

With a quiet sigh, Michael deliberately ignored Joanna's words, as he had so many times in the past. He knew she *thought* she was capable of taking care of herself, but she was a woman with no family and no husband. By all accounts, she was alone in the world. That fact by itself would have made her vulnerable in his eyes, but the fact that she was very pregnant only added to his dismay.

Joanna needed someone to look out for her whether she knew it or not. He had a feeling she did know it, but for some reason he had yet been able to figure out, she'd stubbornly refused to give him an inch or even accept the idea. She clung to her independence as if it was a cloak of protection, deliberately refusing to accept or ask for anyone's help—especially his.

He hated to admit in the past couple of months he'd become idly curious about it. What, he'd wondered, had made her so wary of life? And why was she so insistent that she didn't need anyone, least of all him? It was hardly the reaction he got from most women. He was almost insulted.

"Joanna, how many times have I told you, if you need anything all you have to do is call?" Michael heaved another exasperated sigh, subtly checking the street out of habit, his gaze skimming up one side and down the other before bringing it back to hers with a concentrated frown.

A splash of sunlight caught the light in her hair, making it glimmer like gold. His fingers itched to touch it. Instead he dropped his hands into his pockets, afraid he might give in to the urge.

Lately, he'd found himself noticing things about Joanna—purely feminine things he probably shouldn't be noticing. The way her blue eyes glinted with humor when something amused her. The way they shadowed with wariness whenever something was bothering her. The way her face relaxed and the tension left her when she was tired and let down her guard, leaving her looking far too beautiful for his peace of mind.

With some effort, Michael schooled his thoughts back to the problem at hand. "If I'm not around you know Danny or Patrick would be here in a flash," he continued. "One of us is always cruising the neighborhood. And if we're not, all you have to do is call the pub and my ma would make sure someone got here on the double." He shook his dark head in dismay. "If Da finds out you've been out roaming by yourself again, lugging groceries around, he'll have my hide."

Joanna couldn't help but smile. The Sullivan family as well as the Sullivan Pub were legendary in the neighborhood. When his father, Jock, had been killed in the line of duty, Michael had stepped into his father's shoes, assuming responsibility not just for his widowed mother, Maeve, and the aging grandfather affectionately called Da, but for his two younger brothers, Danny and Patrick, as well as Sullivan's Pub, the family business and neighborhood legend that had been in the Sullivan family for over fifty years.

The Sullivans were a large, close, boisterous family. They fought and they argued and they one-upped one another, but let anyone come between them and they'd risk the wrath of them all. The Sullivans were exactly what Joanna had always thought a family should be.

An old pain gnawed at her, and her hand protectively went to her stomach. Sometimes when she thought of Michael's family she felt a deep, aching loneliness that left her raw. A loneliness from the past she thought she'd conquered years ago. It bothered her to know she hadn't. Maybe because of her condition and her circumstances, those old feelings and yearnings were much closer to the surface.

Absently she rubbed a hand over her belly, feeling a possessive surge of love. *Her* child would be part of a family, even if it was just the two of them. *Her* child would know what it felt like to belong, to be loved, to be a part of something wonderful, she thought fiercely, blinking away the flash of tears that had surfaced out of nowhere as they so often did these days.

A family.

She'd see to it.

"Michael," Joanna said, struggling to hold onto her patience and the bag all at the same time, blinking so he couldn't see her tears. "What I needed today was something not even you or your brothers could have gotten for me."

That caused him pause. His eyes widened and he glanced at her bag suspiciously, as if it might contain a cache of contraband, or worse, some ultrafeminine female thing that would no doubt embarrass him to death. His hold on the bag loosened a bit and he shifted nervously, his gaze sliding from the suspect bag to hers.

"And what, uh, exactly…was it that you needed, Joanna?" he asked in a voice that made it clear he probably didn't want to know.

"Fresh air," she said with a grin as she turned and headed up the stairs again with her bag firmly in tow. She hadn't even cleared the first step before he was next to her, effortlessly slipping the bag of groceries from her arm to his.

"Fresh air, huh?" he asked, juggling the bag. "Seems

to me air is getting much heavier than it used to be.'' Shaking his head, he shifted the bag again, then put his other hand around her elbow, guiding her up the stairs, the way one might do to an aging, doddering aunt.

His devilishly sexy grin remained firmly intact and Joanna was absolutely certain that grin was what caused women everywhere to lose their senses, never mind their inhibitions whenever Michael or his incredibly gorgeous brothers were around.

It totally amused her, grateful she was immune to devilishly good looks and unfailing male charm. Those qualities had the ability to blind you to reality. Especially where a man was concerned.

"Joanna, are you sure you're...all right?'' Michael stopped on a stair and lifted a worried hand to push a stray strand of hair from her face, surveying her carefully.

Her normally peaches-and-cream complexion was flushed pink from the brisk March wind. Her long, golden blond hair was tossed haphazardly around her face, giving her a slightly disheveled look. Those blue eyes, which were both sad and wary, looked as if they were glinting with tears, only making Michael's worry increase.

In all these months, he'd never seen Joanna cry. As his mother had done when she'd been prematurely widowed, Joanna had gathered her strength and simply gone about the business of living, making a life for herself and her soon-to-be-born child. He had to admit he admired her strength and courage.

But he knew her well enough now to know that if she was close to tears, something was very wrong. She wasn't a woman who cried often, not even in her condition. A warning bell went off inside his head and his protective instincts went on full-scale alert.

The urge to take Joanna in his arms and hold her, comfort her was so strong it rocked him. He wanted to do something—anything—to erase the tears in her eyes and the sadness on her face.

His thoughts scared the hell out of him.

It had been a long, long time since he'd felt those purely masculine primal protection instincts for a woman.

For as long as he could remember, he'd done his level best to keep women at bay. Oh, not physically of course. He was a normal, healthy male and enjoyed his fair share, actually *more* than his fair share, of female attention. But he'd never allowed any of the females to get close to him or touch him emotionally. He couldn't allow it.

He had too many responsibilities on his shoulders to ever lose his head over a woman. He had to keep a clear mind in order to take care of his responsibilities and his obligations. It was one of the first rules of life his late father had ever taught him.

He'd only forgotten that rule once. Just once. But the guilt he'd carried with him since that time was more than enough to be a constant reminder of what could and *would* happen when a man let his emotions, especially about a woman, cloud his brain.

"I'm fine, Michael. Absolutely fine." She glanced at him in annoyance, frowning to cover the sheen of tears. These days her hormones and her emotions were constantly shifting, surprising her with their depths. One moment she was near giddy. The next teary-eyed. "Don't you have some bad guys to chase or something?"

He relieved her of her keys and opened the apartment door. "Nope. Not a one. Scared them all away," he teased, ushering her inside, closing and locking the door firmly behind her.

Still carrying the grocery bag, he headed into the cheery yellow kitchen, setting the bag down on the table as Joanna peeled off her spring jacket and dropped into a kitchen chair with a weary sigh, wiggling her aching toes.

"Okay, now let's see what was so important you had to go trotting off to the store all by yourself this afternoon." He opened the bag and peeked in. Just as he stuck his hand in to retrieve something, Joanna jumped to her feet, nearly breaking his fingers as she snatched the bag from his grip.

"There's nothing really important, Michael." Hugging the bag tight to her, she avoided his gaze as her face flushed beet red. A dastardly habit she'd never outgrown.

One dark brow rose and Michael looked at her curiously. "Nothing important, huh?" Amused, he lifted a finger to rub his brow. "I know that guilty flush, Joanna." She only flushed deeper as his gaze went to the bag she was now crushing to her for dear life. "Come on, give it up. What have you got in there?"

"Nothing," she lied. Defiant, her chin lifted. "Besides, I'm perfectly capable of walking a few blocks to the store to get some necessary supplies." She wiggled her toes again. Her tennis shoes were getting too tight, pinching her toes again.

"A few blocks?" Hands on hips, he studied her. "May I remind you that Mick's Grocery is *five* blocks away," he accused, as if she'd just confessed to walking cross-country. Barefoot.

"So?" Cocking her head, she lifted a brow, then set the bag down again. "And do you have a point to make, Lieutenant? Or are you merely giving me a geography lesson here?"

"That's five blocks there, and five blocks back. What if you got tired?" Crossing his arms across his broad chest, Michael scowled, searching his mind for the numerous dastardly acts he was certain could befall her. "Or felt faint?"

Joanna rolled her eyes toward the heavens. "Michael, I've never fainted in my life."

"There's always a first time," he countered, knowing one thing you could count on with pregnant women was that you couldn't count on anything. He didn't have any sisters, but he'd been a cop long enough to know all the things that could happen to a pregnant lady. All of which made him incredibly nervous.

"Although," she said, grabbing his arm for balance as she kicked off her tennis shoes to free her aching toes. "Now that you mention it, there was this guy—"

"What guy?" His voice thundered around the room as his eyes narrowed and darkened. His big body tensed, primed and poised to pounce on anything or anyone who had even dared to disturb her breathing space. She had a feeling he'd be reaching for his gun any second.

"The guy who offered to carry my groceries, Michael," she said dryly, trying not to be amused as she watched his face and body relax.

"So why didn't you let him?" Michael asked, clearly annoyed.

"Oh, my word," Joanna grumbled. Enough was enough. Calling up a little annoyance of her own, she pressed a hand against the broad width of his chest. "Now listen to me, Michael Patrick Sullivan." She took a step closer until they were toe to toe, but she had to tilt her head back to glare up at him. "How many times do I have to tell you, I am pregnant, *not* stupid or incompetent." She thumped his broad chest. "One does not necessarily indicate the others, and in spite of what you might think there is a difference. Every year millions of women all over the world carry children, some with no more effort than they carry a glass of water. I'm a big girl, perfectly capable of taking care of myself by myself. Do you understand?"

One dark brow quirked in amusement. "Big?" He let loose that wicked grin. *"Big?"* He patted the top of her head. The difference in their sizes was a constant source of amusement to him. She couldn't help it if he was the size of a skyscraper, while she was merely…a fireplug. "Honey," he said, trying without success not to laugh. "You've got a long, long way to go before anyone could call you big."

"Size is not indicative of ability, Michael," she muttered, trying to bank her annoyance. Clearly he didn't understand why it was so important for her to stand on her own two feet, to know without a doubt that she and she alone was capable of taking care of herself and her unborn child. It was the most important task she'd ever undertaken.

From the moment she'd learned she was pregnant, she'd known that she'd have to raise and give birth to this child alone. Brian had made that absolutely clear. It certainly wasn't what she'd planned when she'd married Brian, but then life had a way of messing up your plans, and you simply had to handle the results the best you could.

But how could she expect Michael to understand? He'd been surrounded by unconditional love, unfailing security and his entire family his whole life. He'd never known what it was like to be alone or unloved. He'd never known what it was like to know you didn't belong anywhere to anyone. Michael had always had the support of a family to back him up or pick him up if he ever stumbled or fell.

She'd never had any of the luxuries of love or family Michael had enjoyed, not even during her brief marriage. Unfortunately she hadn't learned the truth about her marriage and her husband until it was far too late.

Looking at Michael, Joanna shook her head. There was no way he'd *ever* be able to understand why this was so important to her.

"I'm fine, Michael," she reassured him with a wan smile, still feeling close to tears and not quite knowing why. "Just a little tired I guess." She glanced up at him with a fierce look. "Don't say it," she warned, recognizing the look on his face. "Just don't say it. I walked to the store, Michael, not to Nairobi."

He swallowed the words of rebuke he was about to utter, then lifted a hand and stroked the hair off her face, tenderly tucking it behind her ear, before tilting her chin up so he could look into her eyes. Something was bothering her. Definitely. He had a feeling he'd have to drag it out of her as usual.

"I spotted the can of Squirt in the bag," he admitted sheepishly. "You're not having morning sickness again, are you?"

She'd suffered terribly during the first few months of her pregnancy. He couldn't believe what her poor body had been put through, but she'd never once complained. He'd have never even known if he hadn't stopped by on his way to work one morning and found her curled up on the floor, hugging the toilet, far too weak to even move.

His immediate reaction had been panic, but then realizing she needed his strength—and not a lecture—he'd merely carried her to bed, gotten her some crackers and Squirt and stayed with her until she'd fallen into an exhausted sleep. The experience had given him a new appreciation for women and what they went through to bear children.

"No, no more morning sickness." She shook her head, knowing no matter what she'd said, he'd still worry unnecessarily. "Just a craving for Squirt."

He didn't like the shadows under her eyes, or the worry in them. "Joanna, why don't I run you over to Doc Summers and let him take a look at you?"

For a moment, Michael felt a flash of guilt. Maybe he'd come down too hard on her about going to the store. But the neighborhood wasn't what it used to be. Gangs had started encroaching, coming closer and closer. Even with the police department just a few short blocks away it worried him.

Just last week, a woman had been mugged on her way home from Mick's, the neighborhood grocer. And Mick's, a fixture in the neighborhood for over thirty years, had been robbed three times in the last year.

So his worry about Joanna wasn't totally irrational. A pregnant woman was obviously an easy target, and the thought of her parading around the neighborhood by herself was enough to cause him alarm.

She shook her head, wanting to roll her eyes again. "No,

thanks, Michael. I don't need a doctor, just a nap." Absently she rubbed her eyes, more tired than she realized. "Besides, I have a doctor's appointment Monday right after work." She held up her hand. "And don't start with me about working, Michael. I've told you before, until Brian's life insurance from the department comes through I don't have a choice."

For some reason there had been a snafu with Brian's life insurance. She'd hoped it would have been worked out by now, giving her some financial security. Unfortunately it hadn't.

Shifting his weight, Michael nodded. "I know, Joanna. I'm not rich, but I've got a little saved and you're more than welcome to it—"

"Michael." She held up her hand. This was something else they'd been over and over again. She'd love the luxury of being able to stay home. She was big and ungainly now, and she tired so easily that at times it was an effort just to get through the day. But she couldn't take Michael's money. It was just another form of dependency. One she wouldn't allow.

"Please, don't think I'm being ungrateful, and please don't think I don't appreciate your generous offer, Michael. I do." Deliberately she softened her voice. "But please understand I simply can't accept it." Shaking her head, she inhaled deeply. "I'll manage. It shouldn't be too much longer now. I talked to the captain last week and he assured me things are finally moving along smoothly."

"Yeah, but—"

"Michael, please?" The pleading tone of her voice stopped him. He wouldn't push, at least not now. He had a feeling she had other things on her mind today.

"All right, then why don't you just tell me what's bothering you?" He looked at her carefully, deciding to just come right out and ask. "Does your traipsing off to the store all alone this afternoon have anything to do with what's bothering you?"

"Michael, I went to the store because I needed to get some things for tonight."

"Tonight?" One brow quirked in confusion and he shook his head. "What's tonight?" His mind immediately went on search, wondering if he'd missed something. No, it was March, her birthday wasn't until June.

"The annual Sullivan's St. Patrick's Day party." Maeve Sullivan's St. Patrick's Day parties were legendary in the neighborhood. Maeve closed for the night, and the whole neighborhood as well as the entire precinct of cops from the 14th District converged for an evening of food, fun and laughter.

"Yeah, so?" Michael shrugged. "What about it?"

"I, uh, have a...date for the party, tonight."

Chapter Two

Joanna couldn't help the grin that slid across her features. Her guardian angel suddenly looked as if she'd just announced she'd discovered a notorious gangster hiding under her bed.

"You have a *what?*" Michael rumbled, nearly shaking the rafters. Shock deepened his already deep voice, making it echo off the walls.

"A date," she said simply. It was really a Declaration of Independence. She wanted Michael to know that she was perfectly capable of taking care of herself. She didn't need him or anyone else, but she simply couldn't get through to him. She was absolutely certain this was the quickest, surest way to let him know she was an independent person, capable of living her life as she saw fit, without the help or support of one large, overbearing male cop.

Michael was staring at her with such dark intensity, Joanna laced her fingers together across her belly and gave him a benign smile. She wasn't certain how he'd react to the news, but judging from his tone of voice and the look on his face, he was not amused.

"You have a date with a *man?*" he bellowed with such disbelief she wanted to whack him.

"No, Michael," she snapped, "with an orangutan I met on the way to the grocery store." Giving him a fierce look she planted her hands on her hips. "Of course with a man." She shrugged, annoyed with herself because she felt the need to explain. "I ran into an old friend on my way to the store and he asked if I was going to Maeve's party and I said no." She frowned a bit "Apparently I'm the only person in the entire world who wasn't going. So he asked if I'd like to come along with him."

"And you said yes?" Michael asked, his voice edging upward in shock.

"Of course, why wouldn't I?"

"But you're…you're…"

"I'm what?" she demanded, her eyes darkening in warning. She took a step closer to him, still glaring up into his face. "I know you might find this hard to believe, Michael, but some men happen to find very pregnant women…attractive." She wished her voice sounded stronger, more positive, but the truth of the matter was she felt like a beached whale.

Thank goodness this wasn't a real date, not in the true sense of the word. She had absolutely no interest in any romantic entanglements, not ever again. But it was nice to have a friend to go out with occasionally, a man with whom she didn't have to worry about all the male/female undercurrents.

Of course, she knew Michael would have taken her anywhere she wanted to go, but that was just the point. She didn't *want* to rely on him. Lately, whenever loneliness swept over her, or the real fear she had when she thought about her circumstances, she'd entertained the fanciful idea of what it would be like to be able to lean on Michael. To just relax and depend on him. To let down her guard and let someone else fight the dragons for a change.

Just knowing it might be a temptation was enough to

frighten her into strengthening her resolve to keep him at bay and her independence intact. Once before she'd let down her guard; she'd trusted a man and his betrayal had left her shattered and nearly devastated.

There was no way she'd ever be so foolish again.

Joanna frowned in thought. There had been something else that had been bothering her lately as well. She and Michael had become friends, but on occasion lately she'd felt those male/female...undercurrents with Michael.

And it scared the heck out of her.

She'd been noticing how gentle his hands were when he accidentally touched her. The way his full lips curved when something amused him. The way his clean, masculine scent seemed to linger in her memory long after he'd gone.

It frightened her terribly. More than the loneliness in her heart, more than the yearning in her soul. She could never allow herself to have those kinds of feelings for a man again.

Especially for Michael.

"A beautiful woman is a beautiful woman whether she's pregnant or not," Michael growled, realizing he didn't like the idea of her going out on a date. "I just don't understand, Joanna." Dragging a shaky hand through his hair, Michael simply stared at her. She'd thrown him for a loop with this. It had come out of nowhere. Since when was Joanna interested in dating?

She'd never said anything to him about this. Not one word and he couldn't help but feel...annoyed. It wasn't something he'd ever thought about, or considered. Michael frowned a bit. Although he wasn't quite certain why. It wasn't that she wasn't beautiful; Joanna was stunning. A fact he hated to admit. A guy would be nuts not to want to go out with her or get to know her better, pregnant or not. So why did the idea make his guts churn?

He wasn't quite certain. But protectiveness and possessiveness warred for control. It wasn't jealousy that was streaking through him like a hot poker, he told himself. It *couldn't* be jealousy.

The emotions rose so swiftly, they startled him and he struggled to battle them back. He knew better than to allow his emotions to cloud his judgment. He had to keep a cool head in order to think clearly. If he didn't, it could be disastrous. A lesson he'd learned the hard way a very long time ago.

Still thinking, still trying to remain calm, Michael crossed his arms across his broad chest, determined to take the bull by the horns and put an end to this...nonsense.

"And exactly who is it that you *think* you're going on this date with?" His voice was deceptively low and civil; only someone who knew him well would know that tone of voice was a warning that an explosion was probably imminent.

"Not *think*, Michael," she said, correcting him firmly, not liking his tone of voice. In spite of his size, in spite of his occupation, and in spite of the fact that Michael wore a rather lethal weapon, she had never, ever been afraid of him. Not even when he occasionally used his scare-the-dickens-out-of-the-bad-guys voice with her. Michael was the gentlest man she'd ever met. "I *am* going on a date."

"Yeah, yeah, I heard that part," he muttered with an impatient wave of his hand. "Now who's the guy?" he asked, wanting to get to the important fact.

"Johnny Baily."

He merely stared at her for a moment. "Johnny Baily," he repeated slowly, wondering if pregnancy affected a woman's reasoning power. "You mean that character who works in the movie theater?"

"He's not a character, Michael," she said a bit huffily. "He's just...lonely."

"I'll bet," he muttered. His thoughts were spinning, already contemplating an action appropriate for this situation. And Johnny. "I'll punch him," he finally muttered, deciding it was the quickest, most logical solution. Turning on his heel, he started toward the door.

How dare Johnny try to take advantage of Joanna in her condition! She was completely and totally vulnerable and to know that some guy was trying to take advantage of the situation made him almost lose his infamous Irish temper. Something he rarely, if ever did.

At the moment, punching Johnny Baily seemed far too good for the man.

"You'll do no such thing, Michael," Joanna scolded, grabbing his arm and trying to rein him back in. "What on earth is wrong with you?" she cried, still trying to hold on to him.

"With *me?*" He whirled on her, eyes blazing. "What the hell has gotten into *you?*" He glared at her, furious and not quite certain why. "Out of the blue you announce you're going on a date, with Johnny Baily no less. The man's a...a..." He was trying to think of a word appropriate enough to call Johnny, but couldn't think of one, at least not one he could say out loud and in front of her.

"Watch it," Joanna warned, her own eyes darkening.

Dragging a hand through his dark hair, Michael blew out a breath, trying to gain some perspective. Knowing Joanna there had to be a reason for this. She didn't do anything without a very good reason.

"Joanna," he began slowly, trying to keep his voice and his emotions under control. He was totally perplexed and confused by her actions. "Why did you agree to go out with Johnny Baily?"

She shrugged. "He asked me," she said simply. Which was the absolute truth.

"So you're going out with the first bozo who asks you?"

She would have laughed if she wasn't so annoyed by his reaction. She took a step closer until they were standing toe to toe. She thumped his chest again to get his attention. "Listen to me, Michael Sullivan. For your information

Johnny Baily is not, I repeat *not,* the first man who has asked me out.''

Pride prevented her from telling him that Mick the grocer, a man who was pushing eighty, had a glass eye and false teeth, to say nothing of seventeen grandkids, had invited her to the latest Disney movie last week.

''Who else? Who *else?*'' he demanded, not giving her a chance to answer. His voice was loud enough to roust the dead. ''And why the hell am I just hearing about all of this now?'' He took a step closer.

As a matter of pride, she didn't back up. She merely glared up at him. ''Michael, what on earth is wrong with you?'' Hands on hips, she resisted the urge to smack him. ''And since when is my social life your business?'' she demanded.

And why on earth was he shouting at her? Michael never shouted. Perplexed by his behavior, she stood on tiptoe and touched his forehead, checking for fever. ''Are you sick?'' She frowned, suddenly worried about *him.* ''Maybe you're the one who needs to see a doctor.''

''This is not funny,'' he said, reaching for her hand and holding on as if he could physically will her to stop this nonsense. ''If you wanted to go to the party, Joanna, why didn't you just say so?'' Clearly confused, he shook his head. ''You know I would have taken you.''

''Oh, my word,'' she muttered in exasperation. He was still holding her hand in the comfortable, friendly way he'd done a hundred times before, but this time, his touch made a shiver shimmy up her spine.

''Michael, for a man who supposedly has so much experience with women, you're remarkably stupid.''

''Stupid!'' His eyes widened, then darkened dangerously as he glowered at her, male pride clearly wounded. ''What are you talking about?'' Never in all his life had anyone ever called him stupid—especially about women!

''Listen to me very, very carefully.'' Joanna spoke slowly as if he were a child. ''I know you might find this hard to believe, but dragging an occasionally tearful, very pregnant woman around with you like an old blanket is not exactly conducive to romance. I shudder to think what your date's reaction would be to having me tag along.''

He shrugged, not seeing the problem. "So I'll cancel my date.''

"You'll do no such thing, Michael. I have no intention of interfering with your social life.''

"But—''

"But nothing.'' Her chin angled as her gaze met his. Hers defiant, his stormy.

He was still holding her hand and for some reason she seemed acutely aware of her hand enclosed in his. She could feel the warmth of his skin radiating against hers. It made her heart thud recklessly, making her slightly breathless. The case of flutters in her tummy sure wasn't the baby kicking. She slid her hand from his and slipped it into the pocket of her jumper, hoping he wouldn't see how nervous she'd become from his touch.

It was just hormones, she assured herself. She certainly couldn't be having this reaction to Michael.

"There's nothing for you to concern yourself about, Michael. I've told you a hundred times, I'm not your responsibility. I'm a grown woman, capable of taking care of myself.''

His jaw tightened as his voice cooled. What he was feeling at the moment had nothing whatsoever to do with responsibilities. Yes, he'd made a dying promise to her late husband to look after her and their child, but that promise had nothing whatsoever to do with what he was feeling.

A vision of Joanna laughing adoringly up into some guy's eyes flashed through his mind, and he had a sudden urge to pummel something.

"I never said you were a responsibility, but you're my friend, and I have a right to worry about you, don't I?''

He'd never told her about his promise to Brian, or what

had gone down the day Brian had died. There was too much guilt, still too much grief. He hadn't yet come to terms with it, not enough to try to explain it to her. What good would it do anyway? She'd been hurt enough by Brian's death. Why hurt her anymore or tarnish her memories?

"That's the whole point, Michael," she said in exasperation. "There's no reason for you to worry." She shrugged. "I think you're making too big a deal over this. It's just a date, Michael. Not a lifetime commitment. A few pleasant hours out with a man—"

"But you'll be alone with him," he sputtered, unable to help himself. His words caused her to grin and she rocked back on her heels.

"Generally when you go out on a date with a man you are alone." She leaned up on tiptoe to whisper in his face, wiggling her brows at him. "But if it will make you feel better, I'll stop by the police station on my way home so you can dust me down for fingerprints."

She tilted her head back to look up at him just as he glowered down at her.

Their eyes met, held. For a moment tension froze the air.

Joanna's breath seemed to stop. Suddenly tense and not knowing why, she licked her incredibly parched lips and watched Michael's gaze widen, then drop to stare at her mouth. Her stomach quivered in a way that had nothing to do with her condition, and everything to do with the fact that she was female and he was male. The feeling was so strong, so elemental, the pulse at the base of her neck quickened.

Michael gazed at her soft, lush mouth. For an instant he wondered what she'd taste like. Tension tore through him and he took a deep breath, steadying his breathing and his nerves as he tried to resist the urge to tug Joanna closer, holding her protectively in his arms as he covered that full, beautiful mouth with his.

Guilt suffused him. What in the hell was the matter with him? Were his brains scrambled? This was Joanna—the woman he'd sworn to look after and protect, not seduce!

Stunned by the tension suddenly stretched taut between them, Joanna pointedly looked at her watch, more flustered than she'd ever been in Michael's company.

"Now, if you don't get out of here and let me get a move on I'll never be ready on time." She turned him around and pointed him toward the door, anxious to get rid of him so she could get control of herself. "So go chase some bad guys and stop worrying about me."

"But—" Michael turned to her, but she gave him another helpful push in the back.

"But nothing, Michael."

"Are you sure you won't reconsider and—"

"I'd rather eat raw eggs for breakfast." She unlocked the door and opened it, pushing him through it. "Now go, Michael, and I'll see you tonight." He stopped to stare at her. "Go!"

Shutting the door firmly in his face, Joanna took a deep breath, then slumped against it, giving in to the self-indulgent tears of loneliness that had been threatening all day.

"Mikey, how come you're looking like seven days of rain?" At seventy-eight, Sean Patrick Sullivan resembled a leprechaun. A big, barrel-chested man with snow-white hair and a mischievous twinkle in his eye, he was affectionately called Da by everyone.

He was also the only person alive ever allowed to call his strapping six-foot-five grandson Mikey.

As he scrubbed the scarred wooden bar of Sullivan's Pub with his ever-present white rag, which had a permanent spot over his left shoulder when it wasn't working the bar, Sean carefully appraised his grandson. Something was troubling the boy. You'd have to be a dunce not to see it.

He felt a wave of paternal love and concern. The boys, as he affectionately referred to his grandsons, had grown up to be fine men. Handsome, too, he thought proudly, scrubbing an ancient spot on the bar. Their father would have been proud of them.

"Got a problem down at the precinct, Mikey?" Da finally asked. Retired after thirty years on the force, Da still had a keen eye and a patient ear when it came to cops. Especially when those cops were his beloved grandsons.

"No, Da," Michael said, nursing a cola and rubbing a hand against his weary face with a long, heartfelt sigh. "Everything down at the precinct is fine. Just fine." He'd stopped at the pub to try to get his bearings, still shaken by his conversation with Joanna.

Da nodded in acknowledgment as he continued wiping down the bar. "Well, then, if it's not work, it has to be a woman."

Michael glanced up at his grandfather in surprise.

"No need to look so shocked, Mikey." Da gave an offended sniff. "I'm old, son, not dead. Aye, I remember how much trouble a woman can cause a man," he said with a wistful nod of remembrance. "I recall looking that same way a time or two in my day. This of course," he hastened to add, "was before I met your beloved grandmother."

Da cast a skilled eye around the bar, which was as familiar to him as his own face. Sullivan's Pub had sat on the same corner in Logan Square for over fifty years. Located a few blocks from the 14th District Police Station, and right under the elevated tracks, it had been a cop's hangout from the day it had opened.

Generally filled with raucous police officers and neighborly neighbors, as well as numerous members of the Sullivan clan, the pub was empty this late in the afternoon. In a few hours they'd close for the party. Preparations had begun days before, and his daughter-in-law, Maeve, had nearly completed all of the work.

He was looking forward to tonight; he always did enjoy a good party. And maybe, if he got a chance, and Maeve and the boys were too busy to notice, he might be able to sneak off and have a few puffs on one of his beloved, yet forbidden cigars and maybe even catch a dance with the fine-looking widow O'Bannion. The thought pleased him and he found his spirits lifting.

"So, Mikey, tell me which one is giving you trouble this time." He grinned as he continued scrubbing down the bar, inching closer and closer to Michael. "The cute blonde with the fondness for those short little skirts made of cowhide? Or maybe the one with the strange hair and the even stranger name?"

"No, Da, it's Joanna," Michael said glumly, taking a sip of cola and frowning because it was now warm.

"Joanna?" Da stopped wiping, a concerned frown etched in his features. "Joanna you say?" He moved down the bar toward Michael. "What is it? Is the lass sick?"

Michael couldn't help but smile at the paternal concern in his grandfather's voice. After Brian's death, knowing Joanna was alone and having a child, but more importantly, knowing what had gone down the day Brian had been killed, and how responsible Michael had felt, his family had closed ranks around him and embraced Joanna as if she were one of their own. It was a move as natural as breathing for the Sullivans.

His brothers treated Joanna like the kid sister they never had, and his mother and grandfather, well, like everyone else Joanna knew, they simply adored her. She'd become the granddaughter Da had never had since the Sullivan men's genes seemed to run only toward males.

Michael shook his head. "No, Da, Joanna's not sick."

"Then what is it, boy?" The scowl between Da's white brows deepened as he came down the bar to stand in front of his grandson, slapping his white rag over his shoulder. "I've not the patience for word games today. What's wrong with the lass?"

"Well, nothing's actually wrong," Michael said hesitantly. "It's just…well…Joanna has a date for the party tonight."

"A date." Wisely, Da gave the announcement pause. "I see," he said, wondering why this news would make his grandson so glum. "And this date, it worries you for some reason, does it?"

"Worries me?" Michael laughed, but the sound held no humor. He wasn't quite certain worry was what he was feeling. But quite frankly, he couldn't put a name on exactly what it was he *was* feeling. Miserable was about the best word to describe it. "She's coming to the party tonight with Johnny Baily."

"Johnny Baily," Da repeated, trying to place the man. He nodded suddenly. "Aye, the lad who works down at the moving picture theater."

Michael nodded glumly. "That's the one."

"I see." Da resumed his wiping. "Any particular reason why she's not coming to the party with you?"

Michael glanced up at his grandfather. "I've, uh, got a date."

Da nodded knowingly. "*Ahhh,* I see, so that's how it is." He kept on wiping. "So you didn't ask Joanna then, is that it?"

"I did after I found out she had a date, but she turned me down."

Da continued his wiping. "A woman who's expecting, son, can be a mite prickly, so I'd mind my step if I were you, boy." He nodded slowly. "Mind your step is all."

"And who is it Michael should be minding his step around now, Da?" With her arms laden with plates of food, Maeve Sullivan pushed through the swinging doors that led from the kitchen into the bar and smiled at her son.

At fifty-six, Maeve was still a beautiful woman. Her rich auburn hair had just a whisper of gray and framed a face her late husband had once told her belonged on a cameo.

Sparkling blue eyes, so like her son's, saw the world with kindness and humor.

"Ma, let me help you." Michael stood, striding over to his mother in two quick, long steps. He relieved her of the platters, putting them down on the double buffet table set up at the back of the bar. Picking up an olive, Michael popped it into his mouth.

"So, Michael, what are you doing here in the middle of the day?" At five foot three, Maeve barely reached her son's shoulders, but she never believed size had anything to do with authority. She had ruled the roost and her boys with a kind word and a firm hand since their father's untimely death.

She had loved Jock from the moment she'd laid eyes on him at the Puck Fair in Dingle County when she was barely sixteen. Jock had been on holiday in Ireland with his family the day they'd met. He'd gone to the annual fair to see how the Irish paid homage to their last king. He'd been talking with a "blocker," a horse trader when Maeve had first laid eyes on him.

The moment their eyes had met, Maeve had known Jock was her destiny, even if Jock hadn't. They'd had a time, they did. But in the end, he realized what she had known all along. They were perfect for each other. Even if it had taken some convincing.

In the end, she'd turned her back on her homeland and family, her pledged match and her preplanned future in order to follow Jock back to America to become his bride. She'd never looked back and never regretted it, not once in the forty years since then.

When Jock had died, a part of her had died with him, but he'd left her their sons, and all the friends and family they'd shared their lives and love with, and she'd always been grateful that she'd had the great love of her life, if only for a little while. She'd been one of the lucky ones and wished no less for her sons.

"Michael?" One auburn brow raised, Maeve wiped her

hands on her crisp white apron as she waited for her son to answer. "Do you have a problem that brought you home in the middle of the day?"

Out of all her sons, Michael was the one she worried about the most, simply because he'd taken his father's death so hard. It was a wonder his strong, steady shoulders hadn't bowed with the weight of responsibility he insisted on carrying in the years since.

"It's Joanna."

"What about her?" Maeve asked carefully, taking a step closer to him. "Is she ill?" she asked with a worried frown. Maeve's maternal instincts were strong and endless, especially when it came to one of their own. She considered Joanna one of the family.

Michael shook his head. "No, Ma. I don't know what's going on with her." Dragging a hand through his hair, Michael started pacing. "You know how she is about accepting any help from anyone, especially me. Now I learn she's coming to the party with Johnny Baily."

"I see." Maeve was thoughtful for a moment. "You don't care for the idea, then?" She smiled up at him because he looked so serious.

"Ma, she's pregnant," he began, but stopped at the look of amusement on his mother's face. "What?" he demanded.

"Aye, but pregnant is not dead, Michael." She shrugged. "You've a date for the festivities, so why shouldn't she?" Amused, she touched his cheek. "Listen to me, son. I know what she's feeling because I've been in her shoes. At least when your father died, I had Da and you boys to comfort me. She has no one. Perhaps she's lonely and feeling a bit out of sorts. Pregnancy has a way of doing that to a woman. If she wants to step out a bit with a man I don't see the harm." She sighed. "It's a lonely world for a woman alone, son."

"She has me," he said fiercely. "If she'd just accept help. I asked her to come to the party with me and she turned me down." He shook his head. "I just don't understand why she's being so stubborn about all of this."

"Aye." Maeve shook her head, understanding the situation perhaps more than her son did. "Perhaps you need to understand something, son. When a woman pledges her life to a man, she learns to lean and depend on him, to trust and share with him. If that man is suddenly gone, you feel alone, bereft, abandoned." Maeve sighed. "It's a difficult task to learn to lean or depend again because the fear that someone will abandon you again is strong, sometimes too strong to ever learn to trust again."

"Did you feel like Dad abandoned you?" he asked quietly, looking at his mother carefully. His mother had never talked to him about this before. He'd never considered the fact that she'd felt abandoned by his father's death. The thought shocked and pained him.

"In a way, son," Maeve answered quietly. "Oh, not deliberately of course, and through no fault of his own. But the reasons didn't change the result. Make no mistake, son, I loved your father and he loved me. When he died, I wanted to follow." She swallowed quickly, the pain still fresh after all these years. "But I had to go on with life, for you and your brothers, and finally, for myself." Smiling, she touched his arm. "I had my family, and from what you've told me, Joanna has none. That in itself is hard, but then add the fact that she's expecting a wee one, and it muddles the pot."

"I've tried to be there for her, Ma." Confused, Michael dragged a hand through his hair.

"Aye, but, Michael, you don't understand that sometimes you can't take on another's responsibility." She looked at him carefully. "I know about your promise to her late husband, Michael, but did it ever occur to you that maybe Joanna doesn't want to be your responsibility? That maybe she's trying to do things on her own, to stand on her own, not just for her sake, but for the child's?"

"But why?" He shook his head. "It doesn't make sense, Ma. She needs someone to look after her."

"That's not for you to decide, son." Maeve paused for a moment. "Let me tell you something about women, Michael. No, don't look like that. Believe it or not I do know a thing or two about women," she added with a smile. Thoughtfully she chose her words. "Sometimes if a woman's been hurt by a man, and hurt badly, she feels the need to know she can carry on herself, without ever needing a man again." Maeve's slender shoulders moved restlessly. "It's a point of pride and self-protection. Needing a man leaves a woman feeling very vulnerable to pain."

"Is that why you never remarried, Ma?" He'd always wondered. His mother had never even had a date that he knew of. Her entire life had been devoted to her family. Until this moment, he'd never given it a thought.

"There's still a wee bit of life in me, Michael, so don't start shoveling dirt on me yet." Amused, she shook her head, then took a deep breath. "I never remarried because to this day I'm still in love with your father. I've never wanted another man." She smiled to cover the ache in her heart. "Your father and I, aye, we had a true and good marriage, Michael, and the memories have kept me going all these long years. But from what you've told me about Joanna's husband, perhaps her memories aren't so pleasant." Her voice softened. "It could make a difference and explain her behavior."

Michael was thoughtful, trying to assimilate everything his mother had said. "Are you saying that maybe Joanna's so reluctant to accept my help simply because she's afraid that if she starts depending on me or leaning on me I'll…abandon her?" The idea was so ludicrous, he almost laughed, but the look on his mother's face stopped him.

"Aye, it's crossed my mind, son." She touched his arm again, letting her fingers linger. "And perhaps it should have crossed yours." Thoughtful, she chose her words carefully so as not to wound her son. "Michael, maybe

Joanna's seeing this Baily boy as a way of showing you that she can take care of herself and handle her life on her own, without any help, especially yours.''

He frowned, trying to understand. ''You means she's doing this just to show me that she doesn't need me or anyone else?''

''Perhaps it's to show herself, Michael. And you,'' she added softly.

''That's the most ridiculous thing I've ever heard.'' Shaking his head, he rubbed his chin. ''But it makes sense.'' His gaze searched his mother's. ''So what do I do about it?''

Maeve smiled. ''Have you tried talking to her about this, son?''

He grinned sheepishly. ''Not exactly. I, uh, just sort of lost my temper.''

''Aye,'' she said with a nod and a smile. ''Just like your father. Harsh words won't solve a problem, Michael, and it's only when you're scared that your words get harsh. You do realize that don't you?''

He nodded glumly. To no one but his mother would he ever admit he was afraid of something.

''And what is it you're afraid of, son?'' She cocked her head, then stood on tiptoe to cradle his chin as she'd done when he was a lad. ''That you'll let her down? Disappoint her? Or perhaps you're afraid you'll not honor your promise to her husband?''

He let out a pent-up sigh, memories from the past clouding his vision. ''All of the above.''

''I see.'' Maeve was thoughtful. ''Michael, you've a kind and good heart, but one day you're going to have to realize you're only human. And human beings are fallible.'' She stroked his cheek, her heart aching for her first-born. ''It wasn't your fault, Michael,'' she said softly, just as she had said so many times in the past. But to no avail, she knew. ''You needed to go off to college, to make a life for yourself. What happened was not your fault nor your responsibility.''

"He's my kid brother, Ma," he said fiercely. "He *was* my responsibility." His jaw tightened and a muscle in his neck throbbed. "I should have been here, Ma. If I had been here maybe I could have prevented it." Dragging a hand through his hair, Michael sighed, trying to block the memories. They came anyway.

He'd been offered a scholarship to Marquette. Because he knew the family needed him, he'd planned on going to one of the local, state colleges, but his senior year in high school he'd fallen madly in love with Lisa Parker, who just happened to be going to Marquette as well.

He knew he shouldn't have left.

Devastated by their father's death, at fifteen, Danny was constantly getting into trouble as a way of acting out his pain, his anger. On more than one occasion, he and Danny had come to blows over his behavior. The more he'd tried to help, the more defiant Danny became.

By the time he'd left for Marquette, he and Danny were no longer speaking. He was fed up with his brother's antics. Fed up with the responsibility that weighed so heavily on his shoulders, and torn between his love for his family and Lisa, he indulged himself in a selfish moment, and turned his back on his brother and his family and left home for Marquette. And Lisa.

Danny continued to go downhill, and before the year was out was heavily entrenched in one of the neighborhood gangs. When Michael had realized how serious the situation was, he'd come home immediately, but it was almost too late to save Danny. The fact that Lisa had broken up with him a month earlier had only increased his guilt and his need to go home to help his family.

It had taken him nearly a year to get Danny out of the gang and back on the right track. A year of pain and anguish for all of them, not to mention danger.

When he'd seen the fear in his mother's eyes and the

worry in Da's, he knew he'd let everyone down. Including his father. He'd known what the family had expected of him; what his father would have expected of him, but he'd ignored his responsibility and let something else, or rather *someone* else, cloud his vision and his judgment.

He'd vowed never to let it happen again, but still carried the guilt with him to this day.

"Michael." His mother's voice broke through his memories. "Everyone has to make their own way, including your brothers. You might not always like the path they choose, but you've got to let them walk on their own. Otherwise, how will they learn?"

He sighed, knowing she wasn't just talking about his brothers. "I know, Ma. I know."

Maeve smiled gently. "But it doesn't hurt to be there to pick them up if they stumble and fall." She waited a moment. "You care for her, then?" She could see the answer in his eyes, on his face when he spoke of Joanna.

"Yeah." He blew out a deep breath. "I care for her." Joanna was his friend and he'd come to care for her deeply the past few months. But he wasn't certain his feelings were just those of a friend now, and it troubled and confused him. His feelings were suddenly all mixed up with his sense of responsibility.

Michael's jaw tightened. He couldn't afford to make a mistake; to let Joanna down. He had to keep a clear head.

"Ma, what should I do?"

Maeve sighed, wishing she could make the path easier for her sons. "Aye, son, I think you need to talk to Joanna, to be honest with her—" She held up her hand as he opened his mouth to protest. "I don't mean about her late husband necessarily. I agree that there's no need to hurt the lass any further, particularly now in her condition. But be honest with her about your thoughts, your feelings, your concerns for her. It's hard to find fault with honesty, son. And if you care for her, then naturally you worry for her.

'Tis not fair for her to worry you if it's not necessary."
Gently she smiled at him. "I think she'd understand that."

Michael thought about it for a moment, then smiled and
leaned down and kissed his mother's cheek. "Thanks,
Ma." He felt better, but he always did when he talked
things over with his mother. "I'll be back early enough to
help out tonight."

She waved a hand in the air. "Everything's done for the
St. Patrick's Day party, Michael. I've been cooking for
days. Just make sure you're not late, and corral your brothers and make sure they're not late, either. We're expecting
a crowd again, and you know it's tradition for all the Sullivans to be here."

"Don't worry, Ma, we'll all be here, and on time." He
kissed her again then headed out the door, thinking about
what his mother had said.

She'd told him things that surprised him, and made him
think. And wonder. Did Joanna feel abandoned because of
Brian's death? It made sense, and might explain her wariness about depending on him.

He wasn't certain, but he was going to talk to her. Definitely. The sooner the better.

With a sigh, Michael slammed out of the pub. Maybe
Joanna had been right about something. Maybe he *was*
incredibly stupid when it came to women!

Chapter Three

Music and laughter spilled into the night. The front door of Sullivan's Pub had been opened to release some of the heat and smoke that had accumulated from the crowd during the long evening. The buffet tables, which had been bulging with food at the beginning of the evening, now looked slightly forlorn, and nearly empty. The authentic Irish band that played annually at the party was winding down. The music was not rousing and foot-stomping now, but slow and melancholy in a way that only true Irish ballads can be.

Taking his shift behind the bar, Michael poured a draft beer then slid it across the bar to a waiting patron, keeping an eye on Joanna. She was standing across the room, talking to his grandfather.

It always made him smile to see Da with Joanna. He wasn't sure she quite knew what to make of his grandfather. Da treated everyone as if they were one of his grandchildren, giving equal installments of advice mixed with criticisms.

A few times he watched Da reverently lay a hand on Joanna's stomach and then saw her answering smile.

"You by yourself, tonight, bro?"

Grinning, Michael shook his head and looked up at his younger brother, Danny. Although he was two inches shorter than Michael, Danny, like Patrick, was nearly a spitting image of his older brother. But Danny's black hair was longer, reaching nearly to his collar and giving him a definite disreputable look in keeping with his undercover work in the Gang Crimes Unit. But his blue eyes were the same. Sullivan eyes, his mother had always told him.

"Nope." Michael nodded toward the dance floor where his date was wrapped around a strapping six-foot-six Hispanic man from the Violent Crimes Unit. Tomas had jet-black hair and fierce, frightening eyes. Tomas's looks were perfect for the Violent Crimes Unit, but they were purely deceiving. Tomas was one of the kindest, gentlest men Michael had ever met.

And incredibly popular with the ladies.

Danny shook his head as he accepted the long-neck bottle of beer Michael passed him. "Looks like you've lost another one to Tomas." Danny grinned. It was a running joke between Michael and Tomas, both of whom were notorious ladies' men. Danny glanced around the dwindling crowd, looking for his own date.

Michael shrugged. "I think she got a little tired of waiting around for me."

A look of concern passed over Danny's features. "Hey, Michael, you could have had me or Patrick relieve you." His face broke into a sheepish grin. "Sorry. Guess I wasn't thinking."

All of the brothers took turns bartending. It was the one chore his mother never did. She cooked, she cleaned, she took care of the customers, but she'd never tended bar, simply because she didn't drink and didn't know diddly about liquor, which struck more than one patron funny.

"Not a problem, Danny." Michael shrugged. "I didn't feel much like partying tonight anyway."

Danny looked at his brother carefully. "Something bugging you?" he asked as he took a long pull on his beer, his eyes never leaving his brother's.

Michael shook his head. "Nah, just not much in the mood for a party." Michael filled another drink order, then glanced at his brother, not wanting to talk about what was really bugging him. "What about you? You alone tonight?" He knew the answer before he asked it, but decided to ask it anyway.

Grinning, Danny tipped the bottle of beer back again. "Me?" Danny leaned an elbow on the bar, then hooked one foot over the metal foot rung. "One of the infamous Sullivan brothers alone on a Saturday night?" Laughing, Danny shook his dark head. "It'll never happen." He tipped his bottle toward a tall, striking brunette engaged in a fierce discussion with their captain. "She's a juvenile probation officer. Licensed to carry a gun."

"A gun?" Michael paused and gaped at his younger brother. "Danny," he said carefully, trying not to grin as he poured a whiskey for another patron and slid it across the bar toward one of the waitresses. "Did it ever occur to you that with your history with women, dating a woman who's legally entitled to carry a gun and knows how to use it might not be such a wise decision?"

Flashing the infamous Sullivan smile, Danny shook his head again. "Why?" Taking another sip of his beer, Danny shrugged. "I don't see a problem. I think it's kind of neat."

"Neat." Michael couldn't help it, he laughed, shaking his head. "Well, let me give you a bit of advice, *bro*, if your 'neat' little date shoots you in the backside for standing her up, or not returning her calls, don't come crying to me."

Laughing, Danny shook his head. "Nah, it'll never happen." His gaze scanned the crowded room. "Women love me, you know that.'' There was no conceit in his voice, merely truth, and Michael couldn't argue with him.

Danny loved women, and women loved him back. To Danny, women were a beautiful, never-ending mystery. One he never stopped trying to unravel.

A very brief marriage in Danny's early twenties had gone horribly sour after a few short months, leaving Danny hurt, bewildered and as slippery as an eel when it came to commitment to women. His relationships never lasted long, which was exactly the way Danny wanted things to stay.

Danny's brows drew together. ''Where's Katie?'' His gaze scanned the room again. ''I haven't seen her all night and Ma was asking about her before.''

''Guess she's still down at the day-care center.''

''On a Saturday night?'' Danny shook his head. ''That kid works too hard.''

''Kid?'' Michael looked at his brother carefully. ''In case you haven't noticed, Danny, Katie is no longer a child. She's twenty-something years old.'' Michael laughed. ''And if you like breathing, I wouldn't ever let Katie hear you call her a kid. She's likely to bean you with a frying pan.''

Sipping his beer, Danny laughed. ''She'll have to catch me first. I could take her when we were kids, and I can still do it now.'' As if to prove it, Danny flexed his muscles. His smile faded a bit as his gaze chased around the room again. ''Michael, I think Ma's worried about her.''

''Ma worries about everyone,'' Michael said reasonably, wondering about the concern on his brother's face. Danny was notoriously easygoing, and had nerves of steel. Nothing ever bothered Danny. He took life as it came and never worried about tomorrow, or anything else for that matter, so his comment about Katie surprised Michael.

''Yeah, I know, but this is different. You know how Ma is about Katie. She's one of our own.''

Katie Wagner had been living with the Sullivans since

she was six years old. Her parents had been Maeve and
Jock's best friends, and when they were killed in a car
accident, Maeve and Jock had taken little Katie in and
raised her as one of their own.

From the moment the little red-haired, doe-eyed child
had arrived, Danny had become her protector. She was the
little sister he never had.

Raised by the Sullivans, Katie had grown up with a
profound sense of social conscience and now ran a day-
care center in the neighborhood, specializing in kids who
were too young for regular day care.

Danny's gaze scanned the room again. "And where's
Da? I haven't see him in a while, either."

Michael grinned, scratching his brow. "He was just
talking to Joanna." He glanced around the smoky bar
again. "My guess is he probably snuck outside with Mrs.
O'Bannion to have a few quick puffs on a cigar."

It was a well-known "secret" that Da still snuck an
occasional puff on his beloved cigars, the ones the doctor
had told him he had to give up. But the family pretended
they didn't notice what he was doing, and Da pretended
he didn't remember what the doctor told him. It all worked
out well in the end.

"So how's Joanna doing?" Danny glanced over his
shoulder at Joanna, then back at his brother, allowing a
patron to elbow him aside to grab a handful of peanuts.

Michael's eyes followed his brother's and he smiled
when he spotted Joanna talking to his captain. The soft
sounds of a haunting Irish ballad drifted through the air.
"She's fine I guess."

"You guess?" Danny looked at him thoughtfully. "I
was a little worried about tonight."

Michael frowned. "Why?"

Danny nodded toward the dwindling crowd. "With so
many cops from the station here I was just worried that
someone might say something about…Brian."

Michael's gaze shot to his brother's. "Oh, Lord." He

blew out a breath. "I never even thought about it." He'd been so caught up in his own worries and concerns, it had completely slipped his mind.

Very few people other than the men in his unit, and his captain, and of course his family, knew the truth about what really happened the day Brian had died. His captain had to know out of necessity; the men in his unit knew simply because they were there when everything went down. And his family simply because he needed someone to confide in. He still had nightmares about that day, was still tormented by his own actions as well as the ultimate outcome.

Since Brian's death, Joanna had avoided the police station, and as far as he knew hadn't seen any of the cops that knew Brian. It wasn't as if Brian had any close friends in the unit. Too many knew the type of man he truly had been.

"God, Danny." Michael dragged a hand through his hair. "I never even thought about it." Now that he had, he realized he'd better do something. Quick. "Take over for me will you?" Michael pulled off the white apron he wore over his jeans and shirt and skirted around the other side of the bar.

He hadn't really spoken to Joanna all night. She'd arrived with Johnny Baily shortly after the festivities began, but with a frown, he realized he hadn't seen Johnny in a while.

Michael made his way through the crowd, just as his date and Tomas sailed out the front door. Michael couldn't help it; he breathed a sigh of relief. He probably should have just canceled with Crystal, but he hadn't had the heart. Nor had he had the time. He'd spent so much time this afternoon thinking about his conversation with his mother, that it had slipped his mind until it was too late to do anything but go through with the date. Apparently she hadn't missed him all that much.

The slow, haunting ballad ended and Michael picked his

way through the crowd, pausing to say hello here and there. When he reached Joanna, she was standing with her back to him, talking to his mother.

When she'd arrived, he'd noticed she was wearing a new dress—or at least new to him. It was a creamy white little number trimmed at the collar and cuffs with bright green in honor of the holiday, no doubt. She wore matching green flat shoes that looked like a perfect match and didn't add any unnecessary pressure to her back. He knew how much her back bothered her these days when she wore heels.

She'd done something different with her hair, too, he thought with a frown. It was caught up in a mass of curls atop her head. But now, most of the pins had come out of her hair, and it was barely holding up. Tendrils of curls spilled down her neck, making him smile.

"Are you having a good time?" he whispered from behind, startling her and making her jump.

"Michael." Pressing a hand to her heart, Joanna turned to him with a grin, glad to see him. She was worried that he was annoyed with her because of what happened between them this afternoon. He seemed to have been avoiding her all evening.

Michael looked at her carefully. Her cheeks were flushed with pleasure and her eyes sparkled. But he could sense the underlying tiredness. But no shock or surprise, and he let loose a sigh of relief. Obviously no one had said anything to her about Brian or he would have known about it.

Joanna's smile bloomed brighter as she felt a sense of relief that he didn't appear upset with her. She hadn't intended to upset or offend him. She merely wanted to make a point. "I'm having a wonderful time, as I was just telling your mother."

"Yes," Maeve said, pointedly looking at Michael. "And I was just telling Joanna that she looks tired, and should probably get off her feet."

"I agree," Michael said with a nod.

The band slipped into another tune, a forlorn Irish ballad that wafted slowly through the room.

Smiling at a guest, Maeve wiped her hands on her once-pristine apron. "Why don't you two have a last dance before the band closes shop for the night?" Maeve squeezed Joanna's hand. "Since Johnny had to leave early I don't want you walking home alone." She glanced at her son. "You'll see she gets home safely, son?"

Laying a hand on Joanna's back, Michael smiled. "Definitely, Ma." Michael guided Joanna to the dance floor, not giving her a chance to protest as he drew her into his arms.

For a moment, Joanna froze. She'd never been in Michael's arms before. She'd always carefully, deliberately kept her distance from him. The past few months she was feeling far too vulnerable, and he was looking far too strong. The urge to just give in and allow herself to lean on him was almost irresistible.

It was definitely a recipe for disaster if she wasn't careful.

As much as she found his constant caring and worrying an annoyance, in some small place inside her battered heart she also found it incredibly, wonderfully endearing. No one had *ever* worried about her, or cared about her the way Michael had and it touched her heart in a way nothing else ever had.

In spite of her feelings, she knew that she couldn't allow herself to be charmed by his behavior. He was being kind because he'd been Brian's friend. It was nothing to do with her personally.

"Hey, relax," Michael coaxed, glancing down at her as he drew her closer. Well, as close as he could considering her condition. He heard her sigh, then felt her body relax against his. "Tired?" he murmured softly. She smelled of something sweet and heavenly and he wondered why he'd never noticed it before. It was an intoxicating scent destined to drive a man crazy.

It was working, he thought as he shifted his weight uncomfortably.

"A little," she admitted quietly, trying to ignore the feel of Michael's warm body against hers. It had been a long, long time since she'd been in a man's arms. She may be pregnant, but she was still a woman. Still had needs, wants and desires.

In spite of her own wariness about men, and Michael in particular, she still felt the need to be held and comforted, especially now when she was feeling so vulnerable and so lonely. For just one brief moment, Joanna's emotions warred. She knew better than to allow herself to give in to these feelings, and yet, she decided to be selfish, to allow herself to do the unthinkable and let down her guard for just a few minutes to enjoy the feel of being held if only for a brief moment.

For some reason in Michael's arms she felt…safe. It was something she'd felt so rarely in her life it seemed like a precious and indulgent luxury, and she decided to simply enjoy it for the moment.

What could it hurt?

"So Johnny had to leave early?" He drew back and glanced down at her face, wondering why she looked a bit panicked. He tightened his hand on hers, liking the way it fit in his.

Because of the difference in their sizes, her head was tucked just under his chin. The scent she wore seemed to be interwoven in her hair. Unable to stop himself, he inhaled deeply, letting the scent infiltrate his breathing space. She smelled of spring and wildflowers. He realized the scent was so pleasant, it was addictive.

"Yes," she said softly. Michael's hand on her back was warm. She could feel it through the thin material of her dress, making a shiver race over her. "Johnny…had a sudden craving for popcorn."

In actuality, Johnny had spotted a cute, pug-nosed red-head, and that was the last she'd seen of him. But she didn't mind. He was just a friend, and she was grateful she'd had a chance to get out tonight, and see what one of Maeve's parties was like for herself.

But after the ruckus she'd created with Michael about her date, she wasn't about to admit that to him.

"So Johnny just up and left you all alone?" Drawing back, Michael stared at her, his eyes dark, his body tense.

Joanna couldn't help it, she grinned, rolling her eyes as she glanced up at him. "Yes, Michael, he left me *all* alone." She glanced around the room. "Pretty darn inconsiderate to leave me all alone in a room filled to the rafters with cops. Cops who have taken an oath to protect and defend." She couldn't help it, her grin widened as she shook her head in mock dismay. "Leaving me all alone and defenseless. My goodness, think what could happen." She brightened, enjoying his annoyance. "I could hurt myself bumping into one of those big, bad cops. Or maybe, I might even choke on one of your mother's wonderful sandwiches. Or—"

"I got the picture," Michael grumbled, pulling her close again, wishing she wasn't quite so amused, and he wasn't quite so annoyed. "Guess this means I won't have to dust you down for prints."

"Well not yet," she teased, glancing up at him. "But it's early yet, who knows what could happen." Subconsciously, she licked her lips and watched Michael's eyes darken even further as they followed the movement of her tongue. It made her heartbeat quicken.

Slowly she took a deep breath and avoided his gaze, off balance because of all these male/female feelings that had suddenly been rearing their head whenever Michael was around.

Being in his arms wasn't helping.

Michael's gaze was steady on Joanna's as he tried to ignore the feelings slamming into him. He wouldn't think about how delectable that mouth of hers looked. Wouldn't think about how right she felt in his arms.

"You just love this don't you?" he asked with a grin.

"What?" She feigned innocence. "Teasing you?" She nodded. "Yes, Michael, I confess. I absolutely love teasing you. But then I'm getting so good at it."

He snarled something under his breath as he pulled her close again, enjoying the feel of the softly feminine roundness of her body. In the months of her pregnancy he'd watched her body grow and change. He'd thought it was the most beautiful thing he'd ever witnessed and it gave him a new appreciation for pregnant women. He'd never realized how true it was that expectant women developed a special glow. But Joanna had.

"And by the way, Lieutenant, exactly where is your date?"

She hated to admit she'd been watching him out of the corner of her eye all evening. He'd been tending bar for most of it. But for the life of her she hadn't been able to pick out his date. Some long, tall, blond number no doubt. That was Michael's style.

"Crystal?" Michael smiled. "Seems she had a pressing engagement—elsewhere."

"Crystal?" Joanna repeated slowly with a raised brow. Crystal? The last two had been Amber and Pearl. Obviously Michael had switched from jewelry to stemware. She wondered how on earth he kept track of them all. Maybe he'd consider giving them numbers. Had to be easier than trying to remember their names.

"What?" Michael frowned.

Joanna laughed, telling herself it wasn't jealousy that she was feeling. Not jealousy at all. Michael had every right to date and see other women.

"Never mind, Michael. It's a...woman thing."

Allowing herself to relax, Joanna wound her arms tighter around Michael's neck, letting her fingers brush against the soft material of his shirt as he gently guided their bodies slowly across the floor.

She closed her eyes and swayed with the music. She could smell his cologne. It was something incredibly masculine, destined to dazzle. And it was working its charm. No wonder women had a hard time staying away from him. She'd seen his lethal charm in action, knew how potent it could be, which only added to her determination to keep her distance, and her wayward thoughts and feelings about him in check.

But for just a few moments, she was going to pretend she was a young, carefree woman, and allow herself the pleasure of being held in the arms of a gorgeous, charming man who held no hint of danger for her.

The tempo of the music changed. It was still soft and forlorn, but now also a bit melancholy. "This music is wonderful," she murmured, letting her head rest on his shoulder. It seemed strong and broad enough for the weariest of heads. It made her sigh. "Sad, but wonderful."

"It's an old Irish ballad about a man who falls in love with a woman he can never have."

"Why?" Her head came up with a frown.

"Because she's pledged to another."

"Pledged?" She frowned, not understanding.

Michael smiled down at her. "In Ireland, clans are still strong and arranged marriages and Wedding Matchers are still popular in some sections, especially among Tinkers."

"Tinkers?"

"Irish gypsies. They're nomads who travel in covered wagons from town to town. A Wedding Matcher has been an integral part of their culture for centuries."

"And what pray tell is a Wedding Matcher?" she asked, certain he was teasing her now.

"Ahhh." Michael grinned. "I should really have Da explain it to you, because he does such a wonderful job of it, but I'll try to do it justice. During the Puck Fair, which is held once a year in Dingle Peninsula in Ireland,

and honors the last great King of Ireland, all the single men and women who are looking to wed, or whose clan has decided it's time for them to wed, attend the fair. The highlight of the fair is the 'matching ceremony.' It's something that's looked forward to and prepared for all year long."

"Like Christmas?"

"Absolutely."

"Go on," she said, totally entranced by his story.

"On the last day of the fair, the 'matching ceremony' is held. All of the 'intended' so to speak form a large circle. Men on the outside, women on the inside. Once the circles are completed, the Wedding Matcher enters the center of the circle. She rings a bell and the men start moving one way, the women another. The Wedding Matcher then slowly walks around the inside of the circle, and tradition dictates that when she 'smells' wedding cake, she stops the circle. Whichever woman is in front of whichever man when she smells the wedding cake are 'pledged.' Their marriage date is then set by the families. And it's a match.''

She looked at him skeptically. "Are you telling me the truth?"

He drew back, trying to look offended. "Would this face lie?"

She laughed. "I'm not sure."

"Well it's the absolute truth." He would have placed his hand over his heart but he didn't want to release her. Holding her was more pleasurable than he'd ever imagined. "They say when a Matcher 'smells' wedding cake it's a match destined and blessed by the heavens." They were still moving slowly across the floor even as the song came to an end.

Joanna paused. "Can anyone else 'smell' this wedding cake?" she asked skeptically, looking for a loophole in his story.

"Nope," Michael said with a shake of his head. "Only

a Matcher. That's why she's so honored and revered by so many clans. She's considered to have some kind of second 'sight' when it comes to matches.''

"That's the most incredible thing you've ever told me, Michael." Joanna started to step back out of Michael's arms, but he held her for a moment, not wanting to let her go. Their eyes met and for a moment the room and its occupants seemed to recede as their gazes held, clung.

Unable to drag her gaze from his, Joanna shivered, feeling the shimmering heat sizzle over her. She shivered from fear, not cold.

Michael had the most beautiful eyes, she thought, wondering why she'd never noticed before. All these months...she'd never noticed his eyes. So beautiful and yet in some ways so sad.

Unable to drag his gaze from hers, Michael stared at her, feeling as if his heart had stopped. He'd never held Joanna in his arms before. He'd thought about it, he realized, but hadn't been willing to admit it to himself. Thought about it at night, when he lay alone in his bed, unable to sleep because the image of her kept crowding his mind.

Lately, during the day, he'd found himself daydreaming about her. He'd be cruising the streets, or sitting in a meeting and all of a sudden his thoughts would be filled with her.

And Michael knew in that instant he was treading on dangerous ground. He had a responsibility to her and her child. He'd made a promise, a promise he intended to keep. Once before, when he'd let his feelings and emotions cloud his judgment, he'd forgotten his responsibilities. And too many people had paid dearly.

He could never let it happen again. Especially not with Joanna. He could never let her down.

"Michael..." Clearly confused by the feelings storming through her, Joanna looked up at him helplessly.

Her mouth was soft and slightly open, making him want

to cover it with his own. To just pull her into his arms and hold and protect her. To kiss her until all her fears and worries were gone.

Wanting to break the spell, he dropped an arm around her shoulder in the same friendly way he'd done hundreds of times, carefully keeping his distance from her.

"Come on," he said softly. "I'll walk you home." Still shaky, Michael led her across the room, anxious to be on firm ground once again.

Chapter Four

With his arm still tucked around Joanna, Michael led her out of the pub and into the night. It was nice out so they'd decided to walk the few blocks to her house.

The wind had died, the air had cooled and darkness had descended. An abundance of stars twinkled in the sky, but the night was surprisingly quiet and desolate. The only disturbance was the occasional sound of a passing car.

They walked along in silence for a moment, each lost in their own thoughts. Then Joanna took a deep, wistful breath. In spite of the odd, awkward moments with Michael, she was feeling more relaxed and at ease than she had in months.

"I love this time of night. It's so quiet and peaceful."

"So do I." Michael glanced down at her. "It's nice to see you relax for a change." He brushed an errant strand of hair off her face. Some of the wariness seemed to have left her eyes. She actually looked…happy. It pleased him.

"I am, Michael. Tonight was really fun. But I can't stop thinking about the story you told me."

"About the matchmaker?"

"Yeah." His hand brushed against hers causing her skin to tingle. His fingers were so warm it surprised her.

"It seems unbelievable in this day and age and yet somehow incredibly romantic."

"That's what that last song was about. A man fell in love with a woman who was matched to another."

"So what happened?" Curious, she slipped her arm through his as they waited for a car to pass so they could cross the street.

"The way Da tells it, the man was so brokenhearted on the night before his love's wedding he stole her away from her camp. They fled across the ocean to America, defying their clans and her match so that they could forever remain together."

She looked at him steadily, her heart pounding wickedly. The air seemed to stop. A dog barked somewhere in the faint distance.

"And did they...live happily ever after?" she whispered, wondering why the air seemed so filled with inexplicable tension. She couldn't seem to pull her gaze from his and all those traitorous female feelings swarmed over her again, startling her.

Michael's gaze locked on hers, calm, steady. "Until death separated them," he answered softly, gently tucking a strand of hair behind her ear and letting his touch linger for a moment.

"That's the most romantic thing I've ever heard," Joanna finally whispered. "It's hard to believe love like that can last a lifetime. That kind of permanence, that kind of love is an anomaly to me."

"Why?" he asked in surprise, taking her hand as they began walking again. "Look at my grandparents and my parents. My grandparents were married over fifty years, until my grandma died, and if my father hadn't been killed, my parents would still be married."

"Do you miss him, Michael?" she asked softly.

Michael was quiet for a long moment. "It seems like it

was a long, long time ago, but, yeah, I still miss him." He blew out a breath. "Sometimes, I have a hard time even remembering exactly what he looked like." He shook his head, clearly dismayed.

"That bothers you?"

"Yeah," Michael finally admitted. Her hand was so soft and warm against his, and he realized he liked the feel of it tucked in his. "His death was…devastating. Absolutely devastating. My brothers were so young, so lost. So was my mother."

There was an odd ache in his voice that not even his words could hide. It had to be just as devastating for him to lose his father. She wondered how he'd carried on. Knowing how close-knit the Sullivans were, it was hard to imagine losing an intricate member without it affecting everyone in the family, especially the children. But then children always suffered when a parent died or was lost to them for some other reason.

Joanna squeezed his hand gently, wanting to offer comfort. "What about you, Michael. You were young, too. Only fifteen."

Michael exhaled a slow, long breath. "Yeah, but I was the oldest and it was different for me."

"Why?" She frowned in the darkness. "Why was it different, Michael? He was your father, too."

"Yeah," Michael said slowly. "But as the oldest I knew it was important that someone step into my dad's shoes. Someone had to become the man of the family and carry on his legacy. I worried that my brothers would forget him, forget what he'd taught us, what he'd meant to us…to the family…" His voice trailed off in the darkness and he glanced away, unable to put into words what his father had meant to *him*. The feelings still seemed too big for mere words to encompass.

He'd never talked to anyone about his father, or how his death had affected him. Never spoke of the loneliness that had walked with him for so long. Never spoke of the tears he'd shed in silence and in secret, or the huge void that had been left.

He didn't know why he was talking about it now. But somehow, with Joanna, it seemed as if it was finally the right time. It seemed *so* right, he didn't question it.

Joanna watched him. His voice was soft, impassioned and so sad, she felt her heart constrict. She was looking at the man, but she could still see the little boy he'd been. The hurt, bewildered little boy who'd lost his father, a father he so clearly adored and needed.

Michael shook his head, lacing his fingers through hers and holding on tightly. "I couldn't let that happen," he said quietly. "I couldn't let my brothers forget him or his memory."

"So that's when you became responsible for the whole world?"

His smile was faint in the darkness. "Yeah, I guess. It wasn't anything deliberate or conscious. Someone had to…take my dad's place and become the man of the family."

"But you weren't a man, Michael." Her voice was soft. "Surely you can understand that. You weren't responsible then or now."

"Yes, I was," he insisted firmly.

"Don't you ever get tired of it?"

"Of what?" He tightened his hold on her hand.

"The responsibility?" She looked at him steadily. "Does it ever get to you? I mean, don't you ever want to just shuck it all and take off for parts unknown and be totally free?"

Michael smiled. "I think that's called running away from your responsibility." He was quiet for a moment. "I did it once. Just once," he specified, glancing at her. She could see his eyes had darkened, and his hand tightened on hers. "It taught me a valuable lesson." Michael took a deep breath. "Until then, I'd felt as if the responsibility was weighing heavily on my shoulders. I wanted so much to do everything right, to be everything for everyone because it was what I thought my father would have expected. I was terrified of letting my dad down." He looked sheepish. "I know that sounds silly, but—"

"No, Michael." She squeezed his hand, wishing she could just put her arms around him and hold him, to give him the same kind of comfort he'd offered to her and so many others so many, many times. She'd never known how much it had cost him. "It doesn't sound silly at all. I understand exactly how you felt."

"Do you?" He sounded unsure as his gaze found hers. "*I* wasn't even certain what I felt." They walked in silence for a moment. When Michael finally spoke, his voice was low and intense.

"I guess I just sort of buried all my feelings and emotions," he finally admitted, realizing until this moment, he'd never actually acknowledged it. "I just didn't think I could deal with them as well as everything else," he added quietly, glancing at her, surprised to find her looking at him intently.

"I understand that, too, Michael," she whispered, "probably better than you'll ever know." She was thoughtful for a moment, choosing her words carefully. "Sometimes, when your feelings and emotions are so overwhelming, so…painful, the only way you can deal with them is to bury them. It's a form of self-protection, a way to stop the hurting. I understand that."

She understood it very well. She, too, had learned to hide and bury her feelings. It had become an old habit, one she'd learned before she'd learned to walk. She knew no other way to protect herself. And unlike Michael, she'd never had anyone to protect her.

It was his turn to glance at her. He had a feeling they weren't just talking about his father. It made him curious, very curious. It was the first glimpse of her past she'd ever given him. And the little morsel only whet his appetite for more. But now wasn't the time. He didn't want her to retreat and pull that cloak of protectiveness over herself. He'd wait for the right time.

"I managed to keep everything together for a couple of years," he said, picking up the thread of his explanation. "And then one day everything seemed to fall apart."

Joanna frowned, unable to even imagine Michael being part of something that fell apart. "What happened?"

"I fell in love." He laughed suddenly. "Or so I thought with all the wisdom of an eighteen-year-old. I was absolutely certain this was it—the real thing. It barely lasted two months," he added with another laugh, "but I didn't know that at the time. Hindsight has excellent vision and wisdom."

He shook his head. "I was incredibly young, and immature, and I felt like I had the weight of the world on my shoulders." He smiled a sad smile in remembrance. "I basically did exactly what you said, turned my back on my family and the responsibility I felt was weighing me down and I ran. I took off and left my mom and the rest of the family to fend for themselves."

He took a deep breath, grateful her hand was still tucked in his. He realized he needed her touch right now. He didn't pause to wonder why.

"The result was not pretty. I'm not proud of myself. I was a complete idiot. I not only hurt myself, but my family as well. Especially my mother and Danny. More important, I let down my father and his memory." His words were calm, soft, but underneath the words she could hear the pain, the shame, the utter despair. It made her throat clog with unshed tears.

"Oh, Michael." His words fell like weights, tugging at her battered heart. Somewhere inside there was still that hurt, bewildered little boy who had too much responsibility and not enough comfort, nor time to grieve or accept that he couldn't do a man's job with a boy's heart.

The urge to gather him close, and hold him until the anguish and the despair were gone was nearly overwhelm-

ing. She'd felt enough emotional pain in her life to rec-
ognize it in another, to know the kind of scars and cobwebs
it left on your battered heart.

His anguish at his imagined misdeed was so palpable
the air fairly throbbed with it. This was another side of
Michael. A side she'd never seen, never imagined. And
the knowledge of the depth of his emotions snuck past her
own barriers and touched and softened her own fragile,
guarded heart.

Michael had always seemed so confident, so totally…in
control. She'd never imagined that he carried such deso-
lation in his heart. She began to suspect that perhaps she'd
misjudged him. If unlike her late husband, there *was* more
to Michael than just a gorgeous, charming facade.

Michael had depth and heart. More importantly, he had
character, and a conscience, things that had always been
inherently important to her. Things her late husband had
been sorely lacking. Things perhaps she hadn't been able
to see in Michael because she'd been blinded by her own
prejudices toward him.

Had she unfairly convicted him for crimes another man
had committed? The thought caused a flash of shame. Had
she been unfair to him? For the first time since she met
Michael she wasn't entirely sure.

She began to look at Michael through new eyes and felt
some of her natural wariness toward him subside. Perhaps
he, too, had learned to build walls to hide his pain and
protect himself from further disappointment. Building
walls was something else she knew a little bit about.

She squeezed his hand and turned to look at him. His
eyes looked haunted and sad, making her heart ache and
her arms yearn to hold him. She wanted very much to erase
that look in his eyes, to erase the memories that seemed
to be tormenting him.

"You can't blame yourself, Michael," she said softly.
"I'm sure no matter what your father was proud of you.
He loved you, Michael. You have to remember that. And

besides, you were only a kid, you certainly can't be blamed—''

"Ah, but that's where you're wrong." They'd reached her apartment and he came to a stop, pulling her down on the step to sit next to him. "It *was* my fault and I was to blame. One thing I've learned is that you have to accept responsibility for your own actions. I take full responsibility. But you know how they say not all ill does you harm? I learned a valuable lesson from that experience. Very valuable.''

"What?" she asked quietly. They were sitting next to each other, hips bumping, shoulders touching, the night wrapping them in darkness. Her hand was still gently cradled in his and it now seemed incredibly...intimate.

He turned to her, smiling slowly. "I learned that when you care about someone, when you love them, responsibility isn't a burden, but simply an extension of that love and caring." He shrugged. "It was a hard lesson to learn, one I've never forgotten." His voice softened, gentled, and she saw another side of him. It was incredible to watch. His eyes had calmed, his face had relaxed, and it seemed as if all the tension had left his body. "When you love someone, anything you do for them or because of them isn't a burden." A dazzling smile touched his lips as he shrugged, still confident in spite of the painful lesson he'd learned at such a young age. "It's just another part of loving them.''

His words echoed in her mind, growing louder and louder as emotions swamped her. She'd thought she'd buried all the yearnings from the past, but his words caused a wild rush of unexpected emotions that caused her eyes to fill. An intense ache of yearning, of loneliness swept over her before she could stop it.

She'd always wondered what it would be like to have someone feel that way about her. To love her with an all-encompassing love that made her presence a gift, not a burden.

It was one of the many things she'd never known, and probably wouldn't ever know, because one first had to be loved that way in order to learn to love that way in return.

She'd learned long ago not to yearn for the things she'd never had. But Michael's words had brought forth all the yearnings she'd so carefully buried so very long ago.

She may never have had it, but her child would, she thought fiercely, feeling an overwhelming surge of maternal love. Her child would never yearn for love or a home or a place to belong. Her child would *know* with absolute certainty what it was like to have that all-encompassing love. Her child would know that its presence, its life was a rare and precious gift, not a burden.

She'd see to it.

Fighting to get her emotions under control, Joanna touched her swollen belly. "I think I understand what you mean, Michael." Her voice was ragged as she tried to talk around the lump in her throat. "The baby...some people would think it's a big responsibility, or even a burden, but it doesn't seem that way to me." She shook her head. "It's never been that to me." Struggling to put her feelings into words, she glanced off into the darkness.

"From the moment I found out I was pregnant, it just seemed like an incredibly wonderful gift I was given."

"Any baby is a gift." Unable to resist, he gently stroked her cheek, wanting to touch her. "A miracle really."

She glanced away, looking down the empty, desolate street, feeling sadness engulf her. "Not everyone feels that way, Michael," she said quietly. She turned to look at him, blinking away her tears. "I envy you, Michael, do you know that?"

"Me?" He looked startled, wondering about her abrupt change in subject matter. He found it odd, as odd as her comment about the baby. "Why?"

"Because of your family." She sighed, tucking her free hand into her pocket. "You guys can be a little overwhelming at times, especially when you're all together, but still I envy you.''

"What about your family?''

She took her time answering. ''I have no idea who my family is. I was abandoned at birth.'' At his startled look, she forced a smile she didn't feel and squeezed his hand for reassurance. The last thing she wanted was his pity or sympathy.

She rarely talked about her past with anyone. It wasn't something she was ashamed of; it merely created embarrassing silences since no one knew what to say. And she didn't want pity, never that. Her past was what it was. She'd accepted it years ago.

''My earliest memories are of a children's home, and then a series of foster homes. One after another until I was eighteen and then too old for foster care.''

Looking at her, Michael felt something akin to a vise squeeze his heart. Her voice was devoid of all emotion, as if the words were echoing down a long, empty tomb. The lack of emotion told him more than words how difficult and devastating this had been for her.

Her words had caused a cold net of dread to slip over him. ''You never had...a home?''

''Not a real home, no.'' Unable to meet his gaze, she stretched out her legs, wiggled her toes. Her new shoes were beginning to pinch. ''I just went from one foster home to another, never really fitting in or belonging anywhere. It seemed like I was little more than cheap household help. Or a free baby-sitter.'' She shrugged as if the memories were of no consequence. ''When I was eighteen I moved out on my own.''

The cold emptiness of her words filled him with an unbearable sadness. He couldn't even imagine what her childhood had been like. His family had always been the backbone of his life; the foundation everything else was built on. He had no idea what kind of person he would have become had he not had his family's love and support.

Abandoned.

She'd been abandoned at birth. He remembered his mother's words from this afternoon, about Brian's death, and how maybe it had left Joanna feeling abandoned. The vise seemed to squeeze his heart tighter until it seemed an effort to breathe.

"I'm sorry. I didn't know." He had a sudden urge to hold her, to give her the support and comfort he'd always known. He had a feeling if he did, though, she'd push him away. He knew her well enough to know she wasn't a person who wanted sympathy.

"There's nothing to be sorry about," she said softly, then shrugged. "It was a long time ago and not really important anymore."

He didn't believe that for a moment. Childhood shaped who you were. It was the history and the experiences that laid the groundwork for who you became as an adult. Your thoughts, your feelings, your beliefs, your values. Knowing this, maybe he understood a little bit why she valued her independence so much. Why it was so important to her not to lean or depend on anyone.

She'd never had that luxury. The luxury of knowing a family's unconditional love. Of knowing and trusting without thought that someone would be there no matter what happened.

Michael's heart suddenly ached for the lonely little child she'd been, and the solitary adult she'd become. She wasn't insisting on being independent because of stubbornness or obstinacy as he'd once thought. It was purely out of necessity. If you never had something, you never expected it. She'd never been able to give her trust to anyone, simply because there'd never been anyone to give it to.

Who had walked her to school, or sat with her when she had nightmares? Or a bellyache? Who had loved and cared for her with an unselfishness that put her needs above all else?

The answer was loud and vibrantly clear in the dark, quiet night.

No one.

The vise squeezed even tighter and Michael's breath shuddered out of him as he thought of his own loud, boisterous family. Of how they may have fought and squabbled, but there was always an abundance of love, of caring, of comfort. And unqualified trust among them. He trusted his mother, his grandfather, his brothers and even Katie with an instinct he'd never questioned because he knew they'd never let him down. That's what a family was: unqualified love, trust and dependability. *Home.*

Something Joanna had never had.

Somehow life had betrayed her.

His own thoughts tormented him. He could see her, a lost, forlorn little girl all alone in a world where she wasn't wanted or loved. She'd merely felt like a burden, a responsibility.

Suddenly so much about her became so clear.

Everyone in Joanna's childhood had let her down. Now he understood why her independence was so vital, so necessary to her. It was a way to prevent anyone from ever letting her down or hurting her again. She didn't want his help or anyone else's because she didn't ever want to feel like a burden or a responsibility to anyone again. The mere thought cut him to the quick and caused all his protective instincts to resurface.

Everything made sense now. He never wanted her to know what kind of man Brian had really been. He prayed she didn't already know.

Michael's fist clenched and he felt a sudden surge of anger at Brian for his lack of caring and his immaturity. He had to have known Joanna's background, her history. So how could he have been the kind of husband he'd been, knowing what she'd already been through?

No, he'd never ask her why she hadn't found that sense of home and love with her husband.

But there was something he did need to know.

He looked at her carefully. "Joanna," he began softly. "Can I ask you something? Something about Brian?"

"Brian?" she asked in surprise. Her nerves seemed to squeal in silent alarm. In all these months since Brian's death, they had never talked about him. It was as if they'd made a silent agreement.

She had no wish to know the details of Brian's death. He died in the line of duty and the cause wouldn't change the result. Nor did she have any wish to discuss her marriage with Michael. She'd never told anyone of the disappointment, the fear, the pain or the shame that had been part of her marriage. Brian had fooled her, and she felt foolish that she'd been so naive.

He was gone now and nothing could change the past, so why bother talking about it? Michael was his friend and she had no wish to tarnish Brian's memory. Doing so would serve no purpose. Besides, no matter what, Brian was still her baby's father.

Taking a deep breath, she let it out slowly. "Yes, Michael," she finally answered, hoping she wouldn't regret it. "You can ask me a question about Brian."

"Joanna when...when Brian died, did you feel like he abandoned you and the baby?"

It felt as if the world had come to a sudden standstill. Joanna found it difficult to breathe, her thoughts scrambling as she tried to think of how to answer Michael. It wasn't the question she'd been expecting. She'd expected a question about their marriage. What could she say? Tears quickly filled her eyes again, hot and damp, and she tried to blink them away, to no avail.

The truth.

The knowledge came suddenly. She simply had to tell him the truth. It would serve no purpose not to, and perhaps, just perhaps, he might be able to understand a bit better why her independence was so very important to her.

"Michael," she began, her voice shaky and soft. "Brian abandoned me and the baby long before he died."

Chapter Five

Everything inside Michael stilled. He felt as if he'd taken an unforeseen punch to the gut. Staggered, he simply stared at Joanna in the darkness.

A sickle of the moon shadowed her features and he could see the glint of tears in her eyes. And something else. The wariness and vulnerability. It roused all his primitive protective instincts once again, making him want to hold her, to shield and protect her from whatever had caused that heart-wrenching look in her eyes.

"What?" He shook his head as if trying to clear it, certain he misunderstood her. "What are you talking about, Joanna?"

She tried to smile but simply couldn't manage it. Unable to stop herself, she clung to his hand, pride and independence be damned. It seemed the only stable safety line she'd ever had and at the moment she needed the strength that seemed to flow from him.

Tears seemed to clog her throat, choking her. She swallowed hard several times trying to swallow around the lump that felt lodged there. Inhaling through her nose, she let her breath out slowly, still clinging tightly to Michael.

"Are you sure you want to hear this?" She swallowed hard.

"Yes." His voice was firm. "Tell me." Sensing she was ill at ease, Michael scooted nearer, dropping his free arm around her shoulder to pull her close.

Sniffling in the darkness, she didn't protest, not this time. She didn't have the strength nor the energy. His touch gave her a measure of confidence and she began.

"The day you came to the house to tell me Brian had been…killed was the first time I'd heard anything about him in over six weeks."

Shocked, a million questions popped into his mind, while just as many questions about the day Brian was killed were answered. He banked the questions for now, staying quiet. There'd be plenty of time later to ask questions, to piece the missing parts of the puzzle together. He wanted to let her continue without interruptions at her own pace, afraid she wouldn't if he didn't.

"Go on."

Lifting a hand, Joanna wiped her tears. "I hadn't seen Brian since the day I told him I was pregnant." She couldn't bear to look at Michael and dropped her gaze to stare at the stairs. "We hadn't planned on getting pregnant, Michael. But somehow, it just happened. At first, when the doctor told me, I was stunned, and then totally delighted.

"It seemed the most miraculous thing that had ever happened to me. I was going to have a child." She smiled sadly, remembering that day, the wonder and awe of it. "My very own child. It was like a dream come true. For the first time in my life I'd have a family—a real family. I can't tell you how I felt." Swallowing, she took a deep breath. "I was so excited I couldn't wait to tell Brian. We had been having some…difficulties, and I had hoped that once he knew about the baby, maybe it would help." Joanna paused to take a deep breath, and Michael tightened his arm around her, wanting to hear the rest, but fearing what was to come.

"That night, when I told Brian we were expecting, he went...berserk. He was absolutely furious." Shaking her head, she dashed at the tears that spilled down her cheeks. "I couldn't understand his reaction. Then he said a baby would cramp his life-style. He had big plans and a baby wasn't part of it. It wasn't...convenient. He accused me of tricking him, of getting pregnant on purpose merely to screw up his life." She dared a glance at Michael. His face was set, his eyes serious. She couldn't ever remember seeing him look so serious before. She wanted to lift a hand to smooth the worry lines from his forehead.

"I didn't get pregnant on purpose, Michael," she whispered. "I would never do something like that, but Brian simply wouldn't believe me." Tears clogged her throat again when she remembered the words he'd flung at her; the misery and pain that had lingered afterward. "He made it very clear—it was either him or the baby. He told me I'd better make a decision fast. Then he slammed out of the house and I...I...never saw him again."

"Oh God." The words tore out of him and he reacted instinctively, reaching for her, pulling her into his arms, holding her tight, tucking her head against his shoulder.

Her words had horrified him and his eyes slid closed as a myriad of emotions surged through him. With every word she'd told him, the rage bubbled quickly, spreading to every part of his being. But he knew he had to control it, bury it, not just for his sake, but for hers.

Her words reverberated in his mind, tearing away at him bit by bit. Emotions churned through him, but he tried to keep a tight rein on his control.

He had known Brian could be lower than dirt, but how could a man not want his own child?

He held Joanna tighter, stroking her hair, crooning softly to her. Her tears, her trembling ripped at his heart.

He'd never understand what had caused Brian to say

and do such terrible things. Children were a blessing. A miracle unlike any other. How could a man turn away from his own flesh and blood?

He thought of the look in Joanna's eyes when she'd told him what Brian had said. He couldn't even begin to imagine what she must have *felt* like when Brian had told her the truth. Even now, months later, the pain was still so fresh in her eyes, in her heart, it caused an ache inside of him. An ache he knew would forever linger. He tightened his arms around her. He could feel the rapid beat of her heart against his. Could feel the slender trembling of her shoulders as she wept.

She was holding herself stiffly, holding on to her pride and her control. Holding onto her independence because she had nothing else and no one else to hold on to. Nothing could have touched him more.

"Come on, Joanna, relax," he coaxed, stroking a hand down her hair. "You have nothing to fear from me. And even mothers need a warm, safe place to rest their weary heads once in a while."

His words seemed to open a dam. With a soft sob, she clung to him, clutching the front of his jacket and burying her face against his chest. All the years of pain, of loss, of loneliness, all the years of love she'd never known, came tumbling out in a torrent of tears.

Michael was strong and warm and felt so safe. In spite of her fear of showing her vulnerabilities, she felt safer with Michael than she'd ever felt with anyone. She knew she couldn't lean on him forever, but just for a moment, it felt wonderful to know he was there, to hold her, to comfort her, to lean on, and she reveled in the feelings, so new, so fresh, so…wondrous.

She'd never known what it felt like before, to have someone there for her. To share and absorb her pain, her tears. The ancient barriers she'd erected so long ago seemed to come tumbling down. She felt a rush of emotions for Michael, so strong, so vibrant they frightened her as much as they amazed her.

Feeling helpless and still stunned, Michael merely held her, stroking her hair, sliding his hands inside the bulk of her coat to stroke her back, letting her feel the warmth of his hands, letting her know he was there.

In the silence, in the dark, he held her close, just letting her cry until she was finally all cried out.

Drained and exhausted, Joanna wiped her damp face with the back of her hands, then took a slow, deep breath before laying her head back down on Michael's chest. She could feel the warmth of his body heat seep into her, comforting her.

It wasn't cold, but she was shivering from the force of emotions that had battered her. Sniffling, she laid a hand on Michael's chest, feeling the soft fabric of his shirt under her hand. Until tonight she'd never realized that in his own way, Michael was wounded, too. They both had their secrets, their pain, and it seemed to have created an invisible bond between them.

"Michael?" Through lashes still damp from her tears, she glanced up at him.

"What, hon?" he whispered in the darkness, brushing her hair off her damp face. Her eyes were a bit swollen and her nose was red, but she'd never looked more beautiful.

"You have no idea how guilty I've felt all these months."

"Guilty?" He looked down at her in confusion. "What the hell do you have to feel guilty about?" Anger surfaced before he could bank it. Not at her, but at Brian and what he had done to her.

"Michael, there was no way…no way I could not have this baby." She lifted her head to look at him, not realizing how close he was. Just inches away. "I loved the baby from the instant I found out I was pregnant. I couldn't even consider what he wanted me to do. It was just out of the question." Tears welled again. "Even if Brian didn't want this baby, I did, Michael. I did."

"God," Michael muttered, lifting a thumb to brush her tears away. How had she lived with all of this? he wondered. How had she handled what Brian had done to her and in her condition yet?

She'd known all along that she'd have to raise this baby alone. Even if Brian had lived he would have abandoned her and their child.

What a bastard!

He'd thought she was courageous before, but now, knowing what she'd gone through, knowing she'd been carrying this around inside of her for all these months only made his admiration for her grow. The frustration and anger he felt toward Brian also grew and intensified. How had he been so blind?

Until now, he'd never realized just how remarkable Joanna was. She'd kept this burden buried close to her heart for all these months, never once uttering a complaint or an ill word about Brian. She'd never once expressed her outrage or her anger at the unfairness of his actions or his words.

"Joanna, you shouldn't have had to choose, or justify your actions or feelings. You did the right thing and you have absolutely nothing to feel guilty about. Nothing," he reaffirmed.

"I couldn't be what Brian wanted or needed," she finally admitted. Putting her feelings, her emotions into words seemed to buffer some of the pain.

"What about what *you* wanted and needed?" Michael demanded. "What about what the baby wanted or needed? It was his child and his responsibility as well." Michael took her chin in his hand. "I want you to listen to me, Joanna. I'm not Brian. What he did was wrong, very wrong. But I'm not at all like him."

"I know that—"

"No, you don't, Joanna." His gaze met hers. He was

still holding her chin, and his thumb gently caressed the soft skin. "If you knew that, then you'd trust me to be your friend, trust me to help you through this time, knowing I wouldn't hurt either you or the baby." He inhaled deeply. The sound was sad and forlorn. "But you don't trust me, Joanna. Not enough."

Her face flamed with shame because she realized he was right. She hadn't trusted him because she was absolutely certain he was just like Brian. Brian had fooled her, too, with his carefree charm and his unfailing good looks.

But this was Michael. And she was beginning to see that they were two separate people.

"I'm sorry," she whispered, lowering her gaze.

"Don't be sorry," Michael responded, still stroking her chin. "I understand now why your independence is so important to you. But you don't ever have to worry that I'll abandon you or let you down. You or the baby. You *can* trust and depend on me. If nothing else the way I feel and treat my family should tell you what kind of man I am."

"But, Michael—"

He pressed a soft, quick kiss to her lips to silence her, stunning them both. "No," he persisted, "you listen. You're pregnant right now, and you're very much alone. Even if you were a stranger, I'd be concerned. Everyone needs someone to depend on at one time or another in their life. It's not a crime, just a fact of life." His hand slid to tenderly cup her cheek. "You can't tell me that at times you don't get tired of carrying this burden all alone. That you don't wish there was someone for you to lean on, to count on, to depend on." His eyes searched hers. "Can you?"

"No," she whispered, close to tears. What he was offering her was a gift, a precious gift, worth more than anything she'd ever been given. But she didn't know if she could accept it.

"Then just relax and let me be there for you, Joanna.

Let me be your friend. The only kind of friend I know
how to be.''

"A good one?" she teased, and he relaxed when he saw
her faint smile.

"I care about you and the baby. You have to know that,
don't you?" He waited for her hesitant nod. "I would
never, ever do anything to hurt either of you. Do you believe me?"

She looked at him for long, steady moments, her heart
pounding in trepidation. She wanted so much to believe
him, wanted so much to soften this blunt edge of loneliness
and fear she'd carried around with her.

But could she do it?

Her eyes slid closed and subconsciously her hand slid
to her belly and she thought about the helpless child that
would soon be depending on her. She'd need her strength
and her resources for the baby. It would be heaven to know
that for the next few months she would have someone to
share her burdens with, someone she could trust and depend on. Someone to be there for her.

Heaven. It would be heaven to accept the precious gift
he was offering.

Joanna swallowed hard, unsure of what she was seeing
in Michael's eyes. "Michael, I do believe that you'd never
hurt me or the baby." She heard his sigh of relief before
she went on. "But my whole life I've always felt like a
burden to someone. All those foster homes... And then
with Brian..." Her voice trailed off and she swallowed
hard. "I care about you, too, and the last thing I would
ever want is to be a burden to you."

"You're not a burden to me." He shook his head. "Not
at all. A burden is something that's forced on you. Remember what I said before? When you care for someone,
anything you do for them or because of them isn't a burden, but merely a form of that caring. I'm doing this because I want to. It's my choice."

What he was saying had nothing to do with the promise

he'd made to Brian, and everything to do with the feelings he'd come to have for Joanna. Feelings that were so strong, they startled and shocked him. But he didn't have time to sort them out right now. His only concern was Joanna.

"Let me be your friend. Just relax and let me be there for you." His thumb stroked her cheek. "Trust me," he whispered. "Please, just trust me."

She was still looking up at him, her face damp with tears and he felt his heart constrict. All his thoughts, feelings and emotions seemed to collide as he waited for her answer. Holding her close, her scent intoxicated him. He tried to ignore the feelings she aroused, tried to keep his emotions clear so that he could honor the promise he'd made to her.

He needed her trust more than he'd ever needed anything in his life and he couldn't let his swirling emotions cloud what he had to do. This was far too important; *she* was far too important. He was terrified he'd let her down.

"Joanna?" His heart seemed to stop beating as he waited for her answer.

She blinked, swallowed, then nodded, saying a quick, silent prayer that she was doing the right thing. "Yes, Michael, I'll...try to trust you."

It wasn't quite what he wanted to hear, but it was a start. A big step in the right direction. He grabbed her close, holding her tight, relaxing when he felt her arms hesitantly steal around him.

"I promise you won't regret it," he whispered, pressing a tender kiss to the silk of her hair. "I won't ever let you down."

But as he said the words, in his heart he knew, on some level, he'd already broken his promise and betrayed her.

Impatient, Michael paced the long length of the doctor's waiting room, which was filled with numerous women in various stages of pregnancy. This afternoon he'd called Joanna at work and asked her if she'd wanted some com-

pany when she went to the doctor. He'd occasionally
driven her over, but he'd never actually stayed with her
before since she hadn't seemed too keen on the idea. But
today, she'd said she'd love some company, thrilling him.

He even offered to take her to dinner afterward. After
working all day, then going to the doctor, he had a feeling
she'd probably be too tired to fix herself something to eat.
He knew if he didn't take her out, she probably wouldn't
bother eating.

In deference to her condition, whenever they went out,
he usually let her pick the restaurant since he knew she
had some difficulty eating specific foods at times. And at
other times, she had intense cravings for things. Michael
smiled in remembrance. Like the night she had a craving
for fettucine Gorgonzola. Not al fredo. Gorgonzola. He had
driven all over the darn city until he'd finally found a
restaurant that served exactly what she'd wanted.

Since Saturday, when they'd talked, he'd done nothing
but think of her, hoping she'd be able to do as she'd said,
and trust him. From her acquiescence about the doctor and
dinner, it looked as though she was truly going to try. It
gave him hope that perhaps she was learning to trust him.

Michael checked his watch again. He had no idea what
the doctor did every month when Joanna went in to see
him, all he knew was that for some reason *this* evening it
was taking far longer than the hour she said it would take,
and he was beginning to worry.

Still pacing, he glanced out the window with a frown.
Dark, gray clouds filled the sky as rain pelted, then slid
down the windows. It was a typical evening in mid-March.
The skies were dark, and the cool wind off the lake had
been blowing all day, making it seem colder and wetter
than it really was. Spring might have been only a month
away, but apparently someone had forgotten to tell Mother
Nature.

Michael rubbed the back of his neck as he paced the
small room, feeling decidedly out of place. There were a

few toddlers playing on the floor, but no other men, making him wonder where all the husbands were.

"Lieutenant Sullivan?"

Michael turned. Dr. Summers's nurse was standing in the hallway leading to the examining rooms.

She smiled at him. "Dr. Summers would like to see you for a moment."

"Me?" Michael frowned, and his heart kicked into triple-time. He reached the nurse in three long strides. "Is something wrong?" He glanced over her head. "Where's Joanna?"

"She's still in the examining room," the woman said, giving his arm a reassuring pat. "If you'd just follow me?"

He did, wondering what the heck was going on. Dr. Summers was the neighborhood obstetrician, just as his father, the senior Dr. Summers, had been before him. In fact, Dr. Summers's father had delivered Michael and all his brothers. Dr. Summers senior and junior had delivered just about all the babies in the neighborhood. Therefore, they were part of the neighborhood, and knew just about everyone in the community.

Dr. Summers knew of Joanna's situation, knew, too, Michael's part in her life. The first time Michael had taken her to the doctor, he'd pulled the doctor aside and given him his card, and told him to call him at the station if anything came up.

The nurse knocked on the closed door a moment before opening it with a smile. Shoeless, but dressed in her regular maternity clothes, Joanna sat on the edge of a table, swinging her legs and scowling. He felt instant relief at the sight of her.

"You all right?" he asked as the nurse quietly slipped out of the room and shut the door behind her. He laid a gentle hand on her shoulder, not liking the scowl on her face.

"Just ducky," she grumbled, still swinging her legs and

not looking at him. Michael tipped her chin up so she'd be forced to look at him. His eyes searched hers.

"What's wrong?" Alarm raced through him. She looked perfectly fine, but that didn't necessarily mean anything with a pregnant woman.

There was something in her eyes he couldn't quite identify. Panic? He wasn't sure. His nerves seemed to tighten in anticipation.

"Come on, fess up. What's the problem?"

Joanna blew out a long breath. "Well, for starters, I can't bend down to put my shoes on."

"That's all?" Laughing in relief, Michael bent and retrieved her tennis shoes, then gently slipped them on, tying them in a double knot so they wouldn't come loose.

"Problem solved," he said, straightening to look at her. "Now what else?"

She lowered her gaze again, not wanting to admit the truth. This latest wrinkle in her life was a problem she certainly hadn't counted on. Life sure had a way of handing you raspberries when you least expected it. And she had all she could do not to let the fear racing through her surface.

"Michael?" The door opened and Dr. Summers breezed in, an open chart in his hand and a smile on his face. "It's good to see you again. How's the family?" He extended his hand and Michael took it.

"Fine, Doc. Everyone's just fine."

"Sorry I missed your mom's party Saturday, but Mrs. Fino's daughter decided to put in an early appearance." He glanced down at the chart in his hands, then looked at Joanna. "Did you tell him?"

"No." She shook her head. "I was just about to when you came in."

"Tell me what?" Michael's gaze shifted from the doctor to Joanna and then back again.

Dr. Summers slowly closed the file. "Michael, Joanna's

blood pressure is elevated, not enough to panic—yet—but enough for me to be concerned about it.''

Michael's brows drew together in a frown, not quite certain what the implications of this were. ''So what can we do about it?''

''*We* can't do anything.'' Pointedly, the doctor looked at Joanna, then his face softened into a smile. ''But Joanna can. She's retaining a bit more water than I like and I'm sure that's part of the reason her pressure is up.'' He glanced at Michael.

''I told her she needs to quit working and spend a little less time on her feet.'' Dr. Summers glanced at Joanna with a smile. ''I'm not going to order complete bed rest. The situation isn't at the point yet.'' He frowned. ''I think if she stays home and stays off her feet as much as possible, watches her diet and salt intake, we should be able to handle this problem without too much effort.'' He glanced at the chart again, his gaze moving slowly over it as he sought information.

''She's only got about eleven weeks to go, twelve at best, but those last weeks can be critical. I don't want her going into premature labor. Although at this point, Michael, to tell you the truth, I'm also concerned about her living alone.'' The doctor frowned a bit. ''She's too far along, and blood pressure can be very volatile. Down one minute, up the next. If something should happen—not that I'm expecting it—'' he added at the look on Michael's face. ''I'd much prefer she not be alone.''

Frustrated, Joanna sighed. ''I told you, Dr. Summers, I can't quit working. It's out of the question and I don't have any choice but to live alone. I'm perfectly capable of—''

''Joanna.'' The tone of Michael's voice snapped her mouth shut with a decided click. Interfering, miserable man, she thought with a sigh, remembering her promise. Michael dragged a shaky hand through his hair, trying to concentrate. ''All right, so if she quits working—''

''Michael,'' she snapped. ''I can't quit working.''

Didn't he hear her? Michael knew her financial situation better than anyone. Working was her only option until Brian's pension and life insurance came through.

And as for being alone, what did the doctor expect her to do, hire a bodyguard to stand over her?

Joanna's chin lifted and her stubborn streak kicked in. She'd always believed you had to play the hand you'd been dealt and at the moment there wasn't much she could do about her circumstances but deal with the hand she'd been given. Just as she had all of her life. She'd figure out a solution to this. Something that wouldn't in any way, shape or form jeopardize her health or the baby's.

Just as soon as she stopped panicking.

The moment the doctor had told her about her blood pressure, she'd felt a sense of dread. She had hoped her pregnancy would be like millions of others, totally uneventful. She hadn't been able to plan for any contingencies simply because of her financial situation.

"All right." Michael took a deep breath, trying to assimilate all the information the doctor had just given him. He was worried—damn worried—not just about Joanna, but the baby as well. And determined to do something about it whether she liked it or not. "If she quits working, stays off her feet and watches her diet, do you think that will correct the blood pressure situation?"

The doctor smiled and laid a reassuring hand on Michael's shoulder. "I'm sure that will go a long way toward lowering her pressure. Keeping her stress level down will help as well, which is why I want her to quit working. I'm going to want to check her every week now, though."

"Every week?" Joanna cried. "Why every week?"

"Because," he said patiently. "I have to keep an eye on that pressure. If it goes up much higher, I'm afraid I'm going to have to put you in the hospital under complete bed rest." He shrugged. "I have no choice."

"We understand," Michael said, speaking for both of them and ignoring the glares she was aiming in his direction. He'd deal with her in a minute. He stuck out his hand. "Don't worry, Doc, I'll see that she does everything she's supposed to." He cast a pointed glance at Joanna. "Whether she wants to or not."

The doctor took his hand and shook it. "Good, Michael. That's what I like to hear." He made a note in his file. "Now, Joanna, I want to see you next Monday. Just call the office to set up a time. If you have any problems in the meantime, I want you to call me at home. You have my number?"

She nodded dully. "I have your number."

"Good," the doctor said with a smile. "Then I'll see you next week." Satisfied he'd gotten his point across, the doctor snapped the file shut and strode from the room.

As soon as the door shut, Joanna turned on Michael. "Are you crazy?" Her voice was mild and there was no bite to her words. She shook her head, scooting her bottom forward on the table so she could hop off. "You know very well I can't quit my job, and you know very well why. How on earth am I going to support myself? And then of course, there is the little problem of my living alone. What do you expect me to do? Hire a neighborhood kid to stand guard over me?"

She was furious, absolutely furious and more frightened than she'd been in her life. She couldn't do anything to jeopardize the baby. The mere thought almost made her cry.

"If need be, we will hire a neighborhood kid to stand guard," Michael said, his mind whirling. When he held out his hand to help her off the table, she scowled, but took it simply because she knew if she didn't she wouldn't be able to get down by herself. He placed his other hand at her waist and eased her off the table, gently holding her until she was safely and sturdily on her feet.

"Michael," she protested, grabbing her purse and deliberately stepping out of his embrace. She was feeling too unsettled right now, too scared, and Michael's strength, his calm, and his arms seemed far too inviting. She had to keep a grip on herself. "Be reasonable."

He crossed his arms over his formidable chest. "I think I'm being very reasonable. The doctor said you have to quit your job, so you're going to have to quit your job. You have to watch your diet and stay off your feet. And," he added when she opened her mouth to protest, "you can't live alone. It's out of the question."

Her eyes blazed, then narrowed. She knew in her heart he was right, but it was her mind that couldn't seem to grasp the practicality of it.

"You're right, Michael. There is no question. Surely you can see I don't have any choice in the matter. I *have* to work, and I *have* to live alone." She shrugged, trying desperately to hide her sudden fear and panic. "It's as simple as that."

"You're right," he said, taking her elbow and ushering her out of the examining room. "There's no question about what we have to do."

"We?" She came to a halt in the middle of the waiting room and turned to him, ignoring the curious looks of the interested, waiting patients. "Michael…" She lowered her voice as he nudged her toward the door to get her moving again. "What do you mean *we*?" He turned to her, resisting the urge to throttle her. She rushed on at the look he shot her. *"I'll* find some compromise, something that won't jeopardize the baby, and still allow me to continue working and yet follow the doctor's orders."

Saying nothing, Michael opened the car door and helped her in, not listening to a word she was saying. "We'll talk about it at dinner," he said firmly, as he slid behind the wheel and started the engine.

"There's nothing to talk—"

"At dinner," he said softly, placing a finger to her lips to silence her. Now, all he had to do was feed her and find a way to convince her what he had in mind could work.

Piece of cake, he thought sourly, looking at her stubborn

expression. If he could convince armed robbers and muggers to surrender, certainly he could convince one stubborn, proud pregnant little waif to be reasonable. He glanced at Joanna again.

He hoped.

"Michael, are you totally out of your mind?" Joanna asked across the table, quite certain now that Michael was. "This idea of yours is preposterous."

Taking a sip of her soda, Joanna glared at him, wondering what was going on in that head of his. He'd taken her to one of her favorite neighborhood Italian restaurants for dinner. He hadn't said a word about the doctor's instructions until after they'd ordered, making her believe he'd forgotten the entire mess. Unfortunately, based on his most recent statement he hadn't.

"Is out of your mind the same as crazy, Joanna?" Picking up a piece of fresh Italian bread, Michael tore a piece of it and chewed thoughtfully.

"What?" She frowned, confused, picking up her own piece of bread. "What do you mean?"

Grinning, he reached up and scratched his eyebrow. "Well, earlier tonight you said I was crazy. Now you want to know if I've lost my mind." He shrugged, enjoying her confusion. "I was just wondering if they were one and the same thing."

"I'm sure they are," she commented, taking another sip of her soda and merely picking at the salad she'd been served. Her appetite seemed to have disappeared after the doctor's announcement. "And don't think stalling's going to work, either, Michael."

"Caught again," he said with a grin, appreciably sniffing the salad he'd been served. "But I figured you might be more receptive once you've had some food in you."

Ignoring her salad, she sighed in exasperation. "Michael, food isn't going to change my mind. I cannot, repeat, I *cannot* move in with you." She shook her head firmly, sending her hair swaying around her as if it were a halo.

His gaze was steady on hers. "And why not? Think about it. It's the only logical, practical solution. You know the Sullivans occupy the entire top floor of the pub. There are five separate apartments up there. One for Ma, one for Da. One for Danny, Patrick and one for me."

He leaned across the table, noting the way the candle bathed her in a soft, golden glow. She looked incredibly beautiful. Even if her eyes were shadowed in fear—a fear he knew she wasn't about to admit. It took all his will-power not to reach across the table and stroke his hand down her cheek in comfort. Instead he reached for his glass of wine and took a sip, deciding to take things one step at a time.

"It really is the perfect and only solution, Joanna." He set his glass down and reached across the table and took her hand. "You can stay in my apartment. There's plenty of room. You can even have your own bedroom and bath. Ma and Da will be there every single day to look after you, then at night I'll be there, or one of my brothers, Katie even offered to help out at night. Someone will always be around in the event of an emergency. The chance of you ever being alone in the Sullivan household is about as rare as snow in Hawaii."

Michael paused as their salads were cleared and their main course served. Music drifted through the air from a jukebox on the other side of the restaurant. The sound was low and muffled, making it difficult to make out the words.

Knowing she was about to start protesting he rushed on. "Then, of course, there is the little problem of your job. I know you need the money, but you'll just have to start your paid maternity leave a little early. That way you'll still have some income to keep up with your bills, and not have to worry." He was thoughtful for a moment. "And if that's not enough to tide you over until Brian's insurance is freed, I've got a little put away."

"Oh, Michael." Touched beyond belief by his generous offer, Joanna chewed her bottom lip to stop the flow of tears that she knew were going to start any minute. Darn hormones! Michael's offer was so kind, so generous, so unbelievably...Michael, she wanted to weep.

He had no idea how much his offer meant to her even if she couldn't accept it. He was as good as his word. Knowing he was there for her was a gift she'd never had, and had never anticipated.

"Don't think I don't appreciate your offer, Michael. I do. It's the sweetest, kindest thing anyone has ever done for me."

The shadows of the candlelight played along the strong angles of his face. Joanna tried to ignore his closeness and concentrate on her conversation and the problem at hand. "But I simply can't accept."

Watching her, Michael laced his fingers through hers and looked at their mingled hands, surprised anew at how fragile she was. And how much he enjoyed touching her.

"But thank you, Michael, from the bottom of my heart." She tried to ignore the warmth that crept over her at his mere touch. Another reason she couldn't accept his offer. She was far too aware of the feelings Michael aroused in her, feelings that made her want things she knew better than to want. She was feeling very vulnerable about her emotions and wasn't quite certain she could handle or control them.

So the mere idea of living with Michael was enough to make her go limp. Being with him every day, sleeping under the same roof, sharing the intimacies of daily life would no doubt only increase her awareness of him, and she had enough things on her plate to handle right now without worrying about her hormones and her emotions getting her into trouble.

His meal momentarily forgotten, Michael looked at her for a long moment, cursing her hardheaded stubbornness.

"Joanna," he said quietly. Too quietly. She glanced up

at him in surprise. "Didn't you hear Dr. Summers? This isn't a whim. This is very, very serious. Are you really going to let your pride and your desire for your independence jeopardize the baby?"

He wasn't playing fair and he knew it. Worse, he didn't care. There was no way he was leaving this restaurant until he'd gotten her to agree to move in with him so that he and his family could keep an eye on her. He'd never be able to rest worrying about her all alone in that apartment. If something happened to either her or the baby he'd never be able to forgive himself.

Hurt by his accusation, Joanna's eyes narrowed. "Michael, I don't think that's fair—"

"Hey, life's not fair, but as you've often told me you have to play the hand you're dealt." He cocked his head, studying her. "Saturday you told me this baby means more to you than anything in the world."

"It does." Annoyed, her gaze searched his.

He shrugged. "Then I don't see that you have a choice here." Low blow again, but he didn't care. What mattered was the result. He had to make sure both she and the baby were safe. "You only have eleven or twelve weeks to go. It's not forever, Joanna, just until the baby is safely born. How do you think I'd feel if something happened to you and the baby, knowing I could have done something to help and didn't?"

"I...I never thought of that," she admitted, feeling awash with guilt.

"Well, think about it. Then think about how *you'd* feel if something happened to the baby and you could have done something to prevent it." Guilt began to plague him as he saw fear cloud her eyes. But he'd do whatever necessary to keep her and her child safe. Even if he did have to rely on guerrilla guilt tactics. "Could you live with that?"

She just stared at him, unable to speak. Oh God. He was making this impossible. She wouldn't do anything to jeopardize her child. If she didn't move in with him, she would be selfishly protecting her own fragile emotional state and growing feelings while ignoring her child's well-being. If she did move in with him, she'd be protecting her child's well-being, but ignoring her own emotional state.

Suddenly the answer was clear and there was no question. Her child's welfare came first. Being a parent meant always putting your child's needs ahead of your own, no matter what the situation or circumstances. Joanna realized she had no choice in the matter.

With a weary sigh, she brushed her hair off her face and glanced at the flickering candle. She'd just have to ignore all the feelings Michael stirred up in her. She wasn't about to risk her child's life because her hormones were going crazy.

"All right, Michael." Her shoulders lifted with a weary sigh. "You're right. For the baby's sake I'll move in with you. But just until I deliver," she specified as a huge grin claimed his mouth.

"That's fine, Joanna." He couldn't stop grinning. "Whatever you want. As soon as we're finished with dinner, we can go back to your place and get you packed. I'll explain things to Mrs. O'Bannion, and tomorrow on my way in I'll stop by and talk to your boss and bring him up-to-date."

"Wait, Michael." She held up her hand. Her head was spinning. Things were suddenly moving too fast. "First things first. What about your family? Don't you think you ought to at least ask them about this?"

She'd never shared a house with anyone but her husband, and Brian was rarely ever home. The idea of sharing a house with not just Michael, but his entire family suddenly felt a bit overwhelming.

"Nope." Confident, Michael shook his head. "Nothing to ask. They're going to be thrilled that you'll be living with us."

One blond brow rose and she looked at him skeptically.

"Thrilled?" Laughing, she shook her head. "I find that hard to believe."

"Don't, it's the truth. If I didn't insist you move in with us, considering the circumstances, my family would be all over me like bees on honey." He shook his head. "That's not even a consideration, so don't even worry about it." He brightened suddenly. "I have an even better idea."

She wasn't certain she liked the mischievous gleam in his eye. "What kind of an idea?" she asked suspiciously.

"For the next oh...say...eleven or twelve weeks, why don't you let *me* worry about things? Consider it a brief vacation, one you sorely need. I'll do all the worrying, and you can do the resting. I think that's a pretty fair trade, don't you?"

Amused and charmed, she cocked her head, totally endeared by his offer, his generosity. She templed her fingers and looked over them at him. "There's just one problem with this...idea of yours, Michael."

His brows drew together thoughtfully. "Yeah, what?" He was pretty sure he'd thought and covered everything.

"What do you get out of the deal? I get to rest, you get to worry. Seems to me that's an unfair trade."

"Do you know how to play Monopoly?" he asked abruptly.

"What?"

"Monopoly. You know real estate barons. Land holdings. Utilities." He leaned closer. "The game, silly. Do you know how to play Monopoly?"

"Of course, but—"

"Then that's what I'll get out of the deal." He took a sip of his wine, inhaling deeply of his angel-hair pasta with marinara sauce. Relaxed now, his appetite had suddenly returned with a vengeance.

"Michael, what does my knowing how to play Monopoly have to do with me moving in with you?"

"Plenty." He lifted a forkful of pasta into his mouth, chewing thoughtfully. Finally he said, "No one in my family or at the station will play with me anymore because I'm so good.'' Wiping his mouth on a napkin he grinned. ''So, if you move in with me, I'll have a new pigeon.'' Pleased with himself, he rubbed his hands together in glee.

''Pigeon?'' Amused, she cocked her head. ''Did you say pigeon?''

''That's what I said.'' His smile was far too smug, far too confident. She was definitely going to have to do something about it.

''I'm afraid, Michael you're going to have to eat those words.''

''Nope.'' He shook his head. ''Never.'' He shoveled another forkful of pasta into his mouth. ''No one's beaten me in over six years.''

''We'll see, Michael.'' She smiled smugly. ''We'll just have to see.''

Michael grunted softly, assurance glinting from his eyes. ''Nothing to see but you losing.'' A wicked smile claimed his lips. ''I think I'm going to enjoy this.''

Thoughtfully, Joanna fingered the rim of her glass, trying not to grin. ''So am I, Michael. So am I.''

Perhaps this wasn't the time to tell him that she'd been the Illinois State Junior Monopoly Champion when she was in high school. She'd only gotten better through the years.

Joanna grinned to herself. Perhaps it might be fun to let Michael find out this little tidbit all on his own.

Chapter Six

"Joanna, why on earth are you saving, never mind using, this suitcase?" Michael asked as he walked into her bedroom. "Surely you can afford a new suitcase, and if you can't, I'll be glad to buy you one."

He held the battered, water-stained, badly discolored brown suitcase with two fingers as if he were afraid it might bite.

They'd returned to her house right after dinner so she could pack up some things. While she gathered some necessary clothing and toiletries, she'd sent him down to her basement storage area to get her suitcase and to explain to Mrs. O'Bannion what was going on.

"I can more than afford a new suitcase," she said taking the offending object out of his hand and opening it on her bed. "But I don't *want* a new suitcase." Carefully she began laying folded clothes into it. "Did you talk to Mrs. O'Bannion?"

He nodded. "All taken care of." He lifted the top of the suitcase and practically sneered at it. "I've seen better things in the trash, hon. What gives?"

"Michael," she said in exasperation, snatching the lid from him so she could continue packing. "You ask too many questions." She glanced up at him, then sighed again, realizing she'd been sharp with him. It was totally unintentional. "I happen to like this suitcase, all right?"

"Okay," he said slowly. "I'll buy that, weird as it seems, but why do you like it? I mean there has to be a reason." He lifted the battered lid again. "It's not exactly what I'd call...attractive." It was downright ugly, not to mention in incredibly deplorable condition. Knowing how meticulous she was about everything, this suitcase business didn't make any sense. Michael shook his head as she snatched the lid away from him again. His gaze went to hers. "So what gives?" He was pushing it and he knew it, but this was just really strange.

"There is a reason," she said evasively, turning from the bed to gather up her night wear and some lingerie.

"But you don't want to tell me?"

She grinned. "Now you've got it."

He shook his head. "I'm think I'm offended," he said, feigning hurt. "And here I thought we were friends. I tell you all my secrets."

She laughed. "Not true, Michael." One brow lifted. "I seem to recall you having a distinct memory lapse about what happened the night you went out with...Amber," she said, hoping she'd gotten the right name and the right woman.

"It was Pearl," he said, correcting her, and then had the good grace to flush uncomfortably. "And it wasn't a...memory lapse...precisely. Just selective recall."

She laughed again. "I'll bet." Placing her hands on her hips she grinned up at him. "Seems to me that must have been one interesting escapade if you've got selective recall about it."

Michael suddenly looked nervous. "Whatever you do, Joanna, don't, I repeat, *don't* mention Pearl to my mother or brothers." He fairly shuddered at the thought. He'd endured nearly a month of teasing from his family after the "Pearl incident" as it was fondly referred to.

"And what about Da?"

Michael grinned. "Who do you think got me out of that mess?"

"It figures. You men stick together."

She walked to her closet and picked out a pair of old, comfortable shoes and her slippers. If she wasn't going to be working, she didn't plan on having to wear anything but her slippers, deciding it might be a good idea to give her aching feet and toes a well-earned rest. Standing, she pressed a hand to her back.

She had done that several times tonight, he noted, and it was making him increasingly nervous. "You all right?" Michael asked with a frown, watching as she paused, then rubbed her back again.

"Fine, Michael. Just a little twinge, nothing to get excited about."

He looked decidedly worried. "How often do you get these little…twinges?"

"Don't start worrying, Michael," she cautioned, rolling her eyes. "Pregnant ladies have all kinds of little twinges, they don't mean—oh!" Her arms opened and she dropped the shoes and slippers and her hand automatically went to her stomach.

"Oh my God, Joanna, what's wrong?" Paling, Michael was at her side in two long strides, grabbing her by the shoulders, definitely not liking the way her face had drained of color.

Still holding her stomach, she took a slow, deep breath. "Michael, give me your hand."

"What?" Still a little shaky, he looked at her blankly, deathly afraid something was about to happen. What, he wasn't sure, but whatever it was, he was almost certain it wasn't good and he wasn't prepared. Cop or no cop. He had no experience delivering babies.

"Your hand." She grabbed his hand and placed it on

her belly. He kept looking at her, wondering what on earth she was doing when he felt it. He yanked his hand away as if he'd touched a live wire.

"What the hell was that?" Frowning at her stomach, he dragged a shaky hand through his hair.

"The baby, Michael," she whispered reverently. "She just kicked me." His eyes widened in awe and Joanna grinned. "She actually kicked me." It was the first time she'd felt the life inside of her; the first time she really knew her baby was alive and well. Her spirits soared as her heart filled with unspeakable love.

"The baby?" he whispered, looking down at her tummy as if he expected a baby-in-full-bloom to magically appear. "She kicked?"

Hesitantly Michael gently laid his hand on her tummy again. Joanna moved it down a few inches.

"Here. She's right here." Standing in silence, they stared at each other, waiting expectantly, totally engrossed in the moment. The look in Joanna's eyes, on her face, made something soft curl around his heart.

A few seconds later, Michael felt another series of light flutters, and then one strong kick that made Joanna's stomach harden. He yanked his hand away again as if he'd been burned.

"My God." He dragged a hand through his hair, stunned by the impact of what he'd just experienced. "Does that…hurt?" Worriedly his eyes searched hers as she laced her fingers across her belly.

"No, not at all." Her voice was so soft, the look on her face so filled with joy and unadulterated love he felt his own emotions swarm.

Needing to touch her, he laid a gentle hand on her cheek, mesmerized by what they'd just shared.

"God, Joanna, it's really…*real*. The baby I mean." Their eyes met and held.

Uncomfortable with the thoughts racing through her mind, and the feelings swamping her from Michael's touch, Joanna glanced away. She had to keep a tight rein on her emotions, especially now.

"The doctor said it could happen anytime now."

She couldn't help herself; she nestled her face against his hand, grateful he was here. His hand gently caressed her cheek as their eyes met and held again. A warmth of tenderness seemed to wrap around them drawing them even closer. The air crackled with tension and Joanna swallowed uncomfortably, trying to get a rein on her emotions.

"Oh, Michael, I can't believe it. I've been waiting so long." She laughed suddenly, laying her hand over his, wanting, needing to feel his touch, momentarily giving in to the feeling, her joy was so great.

There were so many things she'd never had anyone to share with, having Michael here to share *this* wondrous moment seemed like a rare and unbelievable gift.

For the past two months the doctor had been telling her to expect to feel movement at anytime. She was getting worried because she hadn't. But he'd assured her it was perfectly normal. And monthly exams as well as an ultrasound had assured both of them that the baby was well. Dr. Summers had told her that perhaps the baby had been moving and she'd simply been too distracted to really feel it.

"Well, it seems like it's been a long time," she added. "Dr. Summers said it could happen anytime now."

"You mean she just started kicking you?"

Shocked by the tumultuous emotions racing through him, Michael slowly withdrew his hand. He hadn't given the baby much thought. Oh, he knew she was carrying a child, but until this moment it hadn't actually seemed like a *real* live little person. Now, since he'd actually felt the life inside of her, he was awed and a bit shaken by how attached he already felt toward the little tyke.

And her mother.

"And why are we calling it a she?" Michael asked with a sudden frown.

"Because it's a girl. I know it, I've always known it." Laughing, she shook her head, amazed, lacing her hands protectively over her tummy again. "Don't ask me how, maybe it's mother's intuition."

"Mother's intuition," he repeated dully. Lord, up until now he'd felt more than capable of handling this expectant mother thing. Now, he wasn't so sure. If the baby was going to be kicking Joanna and doing who knew what else... Michael's thoughts fragmented and he swallowed hard, realizing maybe he wasn't as prepared for this role as he'd thought.

He sure hoped the library had some books about this, otherwise he feared he might be absolutely useless to Joanna, and the baby. He believed in being prepared for any situation, and he clearly needed more preparation to handle *this* situation.

"Is it dangerous? I mean, for you? All that kicking I mean," he asked with a frown, making Joanna laugh again.

"Not at all. It's perfectly natural," she said at the worried look on his face. She touched his arm to reassure him. He was so dear. So incredibly, wonderfully dear. "Really, Michael. Don't worry, I'm fine. The baby just picked tonight to become active." Maybe that's why her back had been aching. Maybe the pressure of the baby moving around had caused the dull ache that had been with her all day.

Not entirely convinced this was a good thing, Michael decided he'd better take some action. Just standing there watching Joanna made him feel utterly helpless.

"You'd better get off your feet. The doctor said you had to stay off your feet." He took her by the shoulders. "Here, sit down." He practically pushed her down on the bed. "I'll finish your packing."

He raced around her bedroom as if the hounds of hell

were biting at his ankles, never once taking his worried eyes off of her. Every few moments he'd stop to ask if she was all right. By the fifth time, Joanna was about out of patience.

"Michael!" She rose to her feet, determined to take this bull by the horns. "Will you stop this?" She relieved him of the bundle of clothes he had crumpled into a ball in his haste, then laid them on the bed. "I'm fine. Perfectly fine. I just went to the doctor today, remember? You were there. If there was anything wrong Dr. Summers would have found it. It's perfectly natural for the baby to kick. And I'm not made of glass. I won't break."

"Are you sure?" he asked, not looking entirely sure himself. She wanted to laugh. She'd never quite seen Michael rattled before. It was both charming and amusing.

"Positive," she assured him. "Now, *you* sit down," she said, pushing him to the bed. "And I'll finish packing before you have a heart attack, not to mention wrinkle everything I own. Sit!" she ordered when he started to get up again. "You're making me nervous. Now sit still and be quiet."

Still shaken, Michael did as he was told, but kept an eagle eye on her. By the time she was finished, and her suitcase loaded into his car, he was wishing for a drink. A long, stiff one. This baby thing was a hell of a lot more complicated than he'd anticipated and he was suddenly *very* worried.

Michael glanced at Joanna. She'd been decidedly quiet since he'd bundled her into the car and seat belted her in. "You all right?" he asked, nervously glancing over at her across the darkened car.

Rolling her eyes, she sighed. "I'm fine. But if you're going to act like a lunatic about this and ask me fifty times a day if I'm all right, I'm going to bean you."

He smiled as he downshifted around a corner. She must

be all right if she was harping. "I'll make you a deal," he said suddenly.

She glanced at him suspiciously. The headlights of the oncoming cars shadowed the elegant angles and planes of his face, making her smile.

"What kind of a deal?" she asked, trying not to stare at his beautiful profile.

He grinned a mischievous grin, wanting to get her mind, and his, off this kicking baby thing. At least until he could ask his mother about it and get some books from the library so he could be certain he was prepared and all of this was perfectly normal.

"I'll tell you about the 'Pearl caper' you've been hearing about if you'll tell why you're so attached to that damn suitcase." He cast a glance over his shoulder at the offending piece, which was nestled on the floor of the back seat.

She deliberated for only a moment, then curiosity won out over her desire for privacy. She'd never had a confidant before, someone to tell the secrets of her soul to. And to her surprise, rather than feeling embarrassed about it, she merely felt…relieved. Perhaps it was because Michael was such a good listener.

"Deal." She grinned, settling herself more comfortably in the car. "But you go first." She frowned rubbing her belly.

"All right." Michael glanced in his rearview mirror before he began speaking. "But let me just say in advance, in my defense, on this Pearl issue, I did absolutely nothing to encourage her or lead her on."

"Uh-huh," she said with a grin, not believing one word of it.

He glanced at her with a scowl. "You don't believe me?"

"Nope." Obviously he had no idea that he didn't have to *do* anything; he just had to be himself. His own natural sweet, charming self. That was more than enough to overwhelm any woman. But apparently Michael wasn't aware of his impact on women.

"Some friend you are," he grumbled. "Anyway, remember we went out just once," he specified, wanting to make his position clear and hoping to stir up some sympathy. "I took her to dinner and then to a Bulls game." He shrugged, keeping his eyes on the road. "No big deal. When I took her home, she invited me in." He glanced at Joanna just in time to see her roll her eyes.

"And?"

"And...well...let's just say the World Wrestling Federation could use her talents." He shook his head at the memory, checking the rearview mirror again before turning down the alley. Because of the changing climate in the neighborhood, he always parked his car in the protected confines of the garage at night.

One brow rose. "You expect me to believe she jumped you?" She was far too amused to hide it. With his size, it would take a female Godzilla to jump him.

"Jumped me?" Laughing he shook his head as he pulled the car into the garage behind the pub and snapped off the engine. He turned to her. They were cocooned in darkness. The early evening rain had finally stopped, leaving the air heavy and damp. The only sound was the occasional car passing by on the side street or crossing the alley. "Let's just say it's a good thing I learned how to run early in life."

"Tell me. All of it," Joanna prodded, tucking her legs under her, giving him all her attention. There was a time when she'd enjoyed listening to Michael's escapades with other women. Now she realized it was a bit...annoying. It shouldn't be—she had no right to be annoyed about his dates—but she suddenly was.

"We'd had a pleasant time, nothing spectacular, and when she invited me in, I went simply because I thought it wouldn't be polite not to walk her to the door at least."

"Of course," she murmured, trying not to grin. "And we all know you're nothing if not polite."

"Right." Turning to face her, he slid his arm across the back of the seat. "I went to kiss her good-night. Just a friendly little peck. Certainly nothing to get excited about." He rubbed a hand across his forehead. A headache had bloomed at the mention of Pearl. "Anyway, the next thing I know she's hanging on me like a poorly hung strip of wallpaper, begging me not to leave her." He shook his head in remembrance. "She had me in a headlock that nearly stunted my growth. It took me fifteen minutes to extricate myself from her."

"A headlock?" Joanna repeated, trying to envision the scene. She couldn't help it, she started laughing at the image of poor Michael being held captive by some lovesick woman. "And I suppose you did nothing to encourage this little scene?"

"Encourage her?" He fairly shuddered at the thought. "Absolutely not. I'm no fool. Like I said it was a date— one date. Not a pledge of eternal love." Dismayed, he shook his head. "By the time I managed to get out of her grasp and out the door, she was naming our children for Pete's sake." He shook his head again. "I ran for my life. And I didn't stop or breathe a comfortable breath until I was home and safely locked in."

"Poor Michael." She couldn't help it, she started laughing. "A victim of his own devastating charm. Again." Shaking her head, she tucked her legs more comfortably under her, then shook her finger at him. "I told you if you weren't careful one of these days one of your little jewels was going to snare you in her trap."

"Nope." He shook his head firmly. "Not me." Smiling, he cocked his head to look at her. Idly he began playing with the soft, golden ends of her hair, utterly fascinated by its softness. "I'm too fast. Besides, no man gets caught unless he wants to."

One brow rose in the darkness. "Is that true or is that

just another one of Sullivan's axioms?'' His hand brushed against the tender skin of her neck and she shivered, trying to ignore the flutter that skipped across her nerve endings.

"You doubt me?'' he quipped with a smile.

"Let's just say I've heard enough Irish blarney out of that mouth to question anything you tell me.''

"I think you just insulted me,'' he said, trying to decide for sure if she had.

"Definitely,'' she agreed with a smile that quickly turned to a frown. "If that's all that happened, how did your mother and brothers find out about it?''

Michael groaned. "That's the worst part. The next day, Pearl called the pub seventeen different times.''

"Oh, my word!'' Joanna shook her head. "There isn't anyone in the world I want to talk to bad enough to call them seventeen times.''

"That's because you're sane,'' he snapped back, still playing with the ends of her hair. He was absolutely certain he'd never felt anything softer.

"What on earth did your mother say?''

"I don't think it's repeatable in front of the baby.'' Gently he patted her tummy with his other hand, letting it linger for a moment, hoping he'd feel another kick. "The fist time Pearl called, she told my mother it was absolutely urgent. My mother had no idea she was a…a…''

"A lovesick lunatic?'' she supplied helpfully.

"Exactly.'' Michael fairly grimaced. "The first time Pearl called the pub, she told my mother it was urgent that she reach me. My ma figured it was police business, and since she knew I was on a stakeout and couldn't be reached, she called Danny at the station, and told him to find me and deliver the message to me personally.''

"And it wasn't?'' she asked curiously. "Urgent I mean?''

Michael exhaled a long sigh, lifting his hand to let it sift through her hair. "Not in the least.'' His gaze met hers. There wasn't anyone else in the world he could tell this story to and feel so comfortable about it. "You know what was so urgent? She wanted to tell me she missed me." He fairly growled the last few words, making Joanna laugh again.

"Oh, my word." Clearly enjoying herself, she shifted her legs for comfort again. "Poor, innocent Michael." She tried to sound sympathetic, but failed miserably.

He grinned in spite of himself, giving her hair a gentle tug. "Yeah, I can tell how sympathetic you are."

"So how did you get rid of her?"

"It wasn't easy. My mom suggested I tell her I had met someone else and it was potentially serious."

"And did you?"

"She said she'd wait," he admitted with a grimace.

"Determined, then?"

"Very, unfortunately. Since she didn't buy that line one bit. Danny, who's always ever so helpful about females, suggested I tell her that I wasn't…interested in women." Shaking his head, Michael shifted uncomfortably. "I wasn't that desperate yet."

"So what did you do?"

"That's where Da came in. Pearl came into the pub one night looking for me. I was hiding out in my apartment upstairs because Mrs. O'Bannion tipped me off that the woman was trying to hunt me down." He grinned a rakish grin. "I'm no fool—I know when to lay low. When Pearl showed up at the pub on her search-and-find mission, Da figured I could use a hand, so he took her aside and talked to her. For almost a year I didn't know what the heck he'd said to her, only that it had done the trick. She stopped chasing after me and I could finally stop hiding."

Not that she wasn't an impressive woman. She was. Gorgeous. Intelligent. Sensual. But he realized he simply wasn't interested.

More importantly, he realized he didn't miss the cat and mouse go-round that went along with casual dating and all the little nuances that went with it.

Curious, Joanna's brows drew together. "So did you ever find out what it was Da told this woman?"

Michael laughed. "Yep. But not until about four months ago. Da finally confessed that he'd told Pearl that I had been seriously contemplating entering the priesthood, and that he and the family felt that her...attentions were too much of a temptation for me, clouding my judgment and making my decision that much more difficult."

Laughing, her eyes widened. "He didn't!"

"He did," Michael confirmed with a smile.

"She didn't actually believe him?" When he nodded his head, she groaned. "Considering your reputation, Michael, I can't believe she bought that story."

"Well she did, thank goodness. I guess Da laid it on pretty thick. And you know how persuasive and protective Da can be when it comes to family. Especially *his* family. That was the last I saw of her."

"Wait until she finds out you have two brothers," Joanna said with a laugh, making Michael groan.

"I never thought of that. Not my problem, though. Danny and Patrick are on their own." He gave her hair a friendly tug. "All right. Your turn." He glanced in the back seat. "What's with that ugly suitcase?"

Because she was suddenly nervous, she unlaced her hands and picked at an invisible piece of lint on her jean overalls. His hand was still on the back of her neck, stroking gently, reminding her how close he was. And how nervous she was. The darkness seemed to wrap around them, creating a fragile thread of trustful intimacy.

"Come on. It can't possibly be as embarrassing as my tale of woe."

She managed a weak smile. "No," she said with a shake of her head. "It's not embarrassing at all." She looked up at him, then realized it would be much easier to talk if she wasn't looking at him, so she averted her gaze.

"I've kept that suitcase, Michael, because it was something from my childhood, and I always wanted it to be a reminder.''

"Remind you of what, hon?" he asked, lowering his voice to match hers.

She managed a glance at him, then sighed. "I've had that suitcase since I was a little girl. It's funny, it's the only thing I ever remember actually owning. I mean, it was the only thing that actually belonged to *me*, and wasn't given to me by an agency or one of the foster homes.'' She hesitated, and he gentled his hand at her neck, caressing the soft skin tenderly.

"And so you kept it all these years?" Now, he understood her attachment to the ugly thing. It made sense. As a child she'd had nothing to call her own, not even a family or a home. Naturally she'd be attached to something, no matter how insignificant, that had been her only possession.

"Yes, but that's not the only reason, Michael." She glanced past him into the darkness and smiled. "Every time I was sent to a new home, I'd pack up that suitcase with whatever little personal possessions I'd been given by the agency or the last foster home I'd been at." She glanced at him, her eyes glinting with determination. "Each time I packed it was like I was packing up my hope as well. Hope that maybe this time I'd finally find a home where I belonged." Because her legs were cramping, she uncurled them and stretched them out for a moment before continuing. She tried to make light of it. "I can't tell you how many times I packed, unpacked and repacked that suitcase, which is why it's such a mess.''

Instinct had him curving his hand around her neck and drawing her near enough to hug her close.

Once again, he felt blessed for the family he had. If he'd never appreciated them before, he did now. Without them, he was certain he would have become a much different person.

As he held her, he didn't say a word; he didn't need to.

He needed her close right now, for his comfort and for her own. He thought for sure she'd protest, but she didn't. They definitely were making progress. He could remember a time when Joanna had shied away from any physical contact. He never really understood why. It always left him curious. He still didn't know or understand why, but it looked as if she was finally getting over it. At least with him.

Joanna laid her head on his shoulder, accepting and savoring the comfort and the caring Michael offered, knowing it was only temporary. But it was all she could handle and allow, and it would have to be enough. Snuggling closer to Michael's warmth, she picked up the threads of her story.

"Please don't look so sad, Michael. It's not sad, not really." She glanced up with him. "I made a vow to myself that I'd never get rid of that suitcase until I found a home, a real home—the one place where I truly belonged. Then I could unpack once and for all and never, ever worry about having to repack or leave again." She felt slightly embarrassed at having revealed so much of herself, but this was Michael she reminded herself, and she had promised she'd try to trust him.

Michael could hear the pain in her voice. The kind of pain that lingered and neither time nor distance diminished. Tension settled in his gut.

The more he learned about her, the more he realized what an incredible person she was. After all she'd been through he would have thought she would have grown hard, bitter. But she hadn't. She'd taken all that pain from her experiences and used it to build a life for herself, a life that allowed her enough hope to love, to marry.

How had she survived? he wondered. She had nothing in the world to call her own but a battered suitcase. His admiration for her grew by leaps and bounds. She had to be strong, tough, to go on, to overcome the imbalance and instability of her childhood in order to become the warm, loving woman she'd become.

And people thought cops had courage.

Joanna had the kind of quiet courage that the average person couldn't even begin to comprehend.

And now she was going to become a mother.

The most draining, selfless role anyone could ever take on. In spite of the circumstances, he knew how much this child meant to her. She didn't have to go through with the pregnancy, but for her there was no question. She'd made the decision based on love.

Joanna may not have had that loving security of a home or family while she was growing up, but he knew without a doubt her own child would never suffer the same fate.

The desire to protect her, to soothe away the years of pain and hurt was so strong it rocked him. He'd always valued his control. As a cop it was an inherent part of his job, his life. But for some reason with Joanna he frequently found his control slipping. She was wiggling her way past all the natural barriers he'd erected toward women and was etching out a place for herself in his heart.

The realization scared him.

He couldn't let his emotions or his growing feelings for her cloud his judgment. Both she and the baby were depending on him. He couldn't let them down. He simply couldn't. The mere thought that it might be a possibility was so frightening, he made a silent vow to put his feelings and emotions on hold, to bury them until he felt certain he could deal with them properly and *not* allow them to interfere with his judgment or what he had to do.

"That's why you kept the suitcase, isn't it?" He continued stroking her hair. "Because you never found that place. A home where you belonged, right?"

"Right." She sighed. Her chin lifted slightly and he saw a trace of pride as well as determination. He knew better than to pity her. She didn't want or need it. "Michael?"

Her voice was hesitant. "I've...I've never told anyone that before. Not even Brian."

He felt humbled as he realized the implication of her words. She'd trusted him with something that she'd never revealed to anyone else.

He brushed his lips across her forehead. "I'm glad you told me, Joanna. It means a lot to me that you trust me enough to confide in me."

She trusted him.

He'd brazenly asked for her trust and she'd somehow given it to him. Perhaps not easily or willingly, but she'd given it just the same. And he knew he could never do anything to shatter that fragile bond of trust, knowing because of her past she'd probably never given it to many people.

For an instant he felt a flash of guilt, wondering if he made the right decision about not telling her about Brian and the circumstances of his death. His intentions had been honorable, truly honorable, but his actions, well, he no longer knew if his decision was a way to protect himself.

Or her.

Michael sighed. Maybe he should have told her long ago about what had happened that day, not to ease his own grief and guilt, but simply because she had a right to know. But he couldn't. Not now, not knowing what he knew about her and her past, and her relationship with Brian before his death. With the medical complications she was facing he didn't want to do anything to increase her stress.

No, he'd done the right thing he realized. And he'd just have to handle any fallout from that decision.

Protecting Joanna and her child was the most important thing.

"Come on. Let's get you in and settled." He reached in the back seat for her suitcase. "I think we've both had enough excitement for one day."

Helping her from the car, Michael prayed that in trying to protect her, he wouldn't ultimately betray her.

Chapter Seven

"I can't believe you're going to beat me again," Michael complained, dragging a hand through his hair. He stared down at the Monopoly game that had been permanently set up on the game table in his living room, ignoring the amused glances Joanna kept shooting in his direction.

"Yes, Michael. Again." She smiled smugly. "I'd say it's the twelfth time in what…the past two weeks?" She couldn't help but gloat. She'd been repeatedly beating him ever since she'd moved in. A fact she never let him forget.

"Yeah, but you have an advantage," he moaned. "I should cry foul."

"And exactly what's my advantage?" she asked with a smile, grabbing a handful of fat-free, salt-free air popped popcorn from the bowl on the table.

She glanced at the popcorn in her hand and tried not to frown. It was just one of Michael's many "ideas" since she'd moved in. He'd stocked his apartment with every kind of health food he could find in an effort to keep her healthy.

Their first trip to the grocery store had been hysterical.

She'd never been grocery shopping with a man before. Brian had eschewed any chores he felt feminine. So going grocery shopping with Michael had been an experience.

His natural tastes ran toward potato chips, cake and beer—until he looked at her as if just remembering she was pregnant. Flushing acutely, he immediately changed directions. Emptying his already full cart, he then proceeded to march up and down the aisles as if he were a man on a mission, nearly toppling their cart with what he considered "healthy" food.

It was enough to make her gag. They had every type of no-fat, no-calorie foodstuff known to man. It would probably take *several* pregnancies to demolish everything he'd bought.

"Being pregnant is an advantage," he conceded, still staring at the board. And then at the pitiful pile of money he had left. "Everyone knows there's something special about pregnant women." His brows drew together. "I think it's that they have special powers or something. At least when it comes to board games."

She laughed, surprised at how good-natured he was about losing. It amazed her how easily and quickly they'd fallen into a pattern and how much fun they had together. She thought it would be difficult, even awkward to live with Michael. But it hadn't been.

Living with him, sharing in his life and activities as well as his family had given her, for the first time in her life, a glimpse of what a normal relationship and family life would be like. It made her yearn again, yearn for the things she'd never had, could never have.

Before she'd had no idea what she'd missed. Now, she did and it made her both happy and deeply sad.

But she was grateful Michael had given her the opportunity, at least for a little while, to experience both him and his family. She kept reminding herself this situation was merely temporary, just until the baby was born and they were both out of danger. She couldn't allow herself to conjure up fanciful dreams of what-if? She'd done that too many times as a child, hoping and yearning for something and someone, only to be brutally disappointed.

Never again would she harbor secret dreams about things she knew she couldn't have. It was a path straight to heartache. She knew better.

But oh, it didn't hurt to fantasize a little.

Sometimes at night she would lay in bed with a hand placed protectively across her belly, wondering what it would be like to have a normal marriage, a family and a relationship. It was a yearning so strong, but no longer just for herself, but her child as well. It was hard to reconcile that her own child would never have that family. Oh, she'd have her, but sometimes Joanna worried that it wouldn't be enough.

The Sullivans had quickly accepted her into their fold, going out of their way to make her feel welcome. Most days she spent with Da who regaled and entertained her for hours with his remembrances of Ireland.

If Da was busy, it was Maeve who spent time with her. They'd taken to going for a walk every afternoon after lunch. As for Danny and Patrick, and even Katie, they merely treated her as if she…belonged. And nothing could have made her happier, or more comfortable.

Knowing she could beat Michael at Monopoly every evening only added icing to the cake.

Blinking, Joanna watched Michael, trying not to grin. "Michael, if you're trying to figure out what a woman's special powers are, let me give you a clue here. They have nothing to do with pregnancy." A grin slid smoothly over her features at his perplexed look. "We're just intellectually superior." She tapped a finger on the board. "Especially when it comes to playing board games with arrogant, insufferable males."

"Low blow," he complained, counting out his remaining money and realizing he was nearly broke. And probably would be beaten again. Michael sighed.

"Are you buying that railroad?" she inquired, pressing a hand to her back and shifting on the chair. It didn't seem possible, but she'd grown even bigger in the past two weeks. The doctor said it was perfectly normal, but it was getting uncomfortable to do simple things like walk and sleep. "Or are you simply going to drool over it?"

"I think drooling is all I can afford," he admitted with a frown.

He glanced up at her, noting the look on her face. Living with her the past two weeks had taught him to pick up on every little nuance. He knew when she was tired, uncomfortable, or even hungry.

He'd never lived with a woman before. He wouldn't have admitted it to anyone, but it had worried him a little. But his worries had been groundless. He and Joanna got along very well. In fact, they were totally, completely compatible. They actually liked being together and never ran out of things to talk about. Funny, other than his mother, he generally didn't talk much with women. His mind was usually on other things.

Living with Joanna—having her here every night when he came home and every morning when he woke up—was turning out to be a very pleasant experience. Something he found he really looked forward to.

"You all right?" he asked, watching her carefully. She was squirming and stretching and pressing a hand to her back the way she did when her back hurt or her muscles were cramping.

"Just my back again." She stretched and arched, trying to work out the kinks. "The baby's more than restless tonight." Wincing, she arched again. The baby had been so active the past few weeks she was absolutely certain the kid was going to go directly from the womb to competitive gymnastics.

Michael glanced at his watch, then out the kitchen window. It was dark and dreary and rain had been falling for almost two days, putting a damp, dark pallor over everything.

"It's almost nine." His brows drew together. "We should probably go for our walk, but it's still raining out." He went to the window, pulled back the blue-and-white checked curtain, then shook his head. "Do you think someone should tell Mother Nature it's April and we're waiting for spring?"

It had been unseasonably cool and wet for early April, making it seem as if winter had been extended indefinitely.

Every evening after dinner, they usually played Monopoly or some other board game. Just the two of them, or with someone from the family. They then went for a walk—weather permitting.

After their walk they usually returned to the house where Michael would light a fire in the fireplace and make hot chocolate to sip while they watched the evening news together. Nothing spectacular or unusual, but fun nevertheless. It had taken him by surprise when he realized anything he did with Joanna seemed fun. She seemed to have filled a void in his life he hadn't even known was there. He realized that he was suddenly looking forward to coming home every night.

He'd done a rather successful job of burying his emotions. It was the only way he could ensure that he do what was necessary for Joanna. There would be time later, he was sure, to sort through all the tumultuous feelings he had, but right now, he knew he had something far more important to do, and he wouldn't let his feelings or emotions cloud his judgment.

He simply couldn't allow it.

For both Joanna and the baby.

Joanna glanced at her own watch, then sighed. "Why don't we just stay in then, Michael?" She pressed her back again, stretching her legs out under the table hoping it would help. "I'm kind of tired tonight anyway."

Leaving the board as it was, Michael was just helping

her to her feet when someone knocked on the door. "Come in," he called, bending to untie her tennis shoes for her. It was one of the small items that she'd finally conceded she actually needed help with.

"Hey, bro—" Patrick, Michael's youngest brother, skidded to a halt, looking at the two of them and then at the game board on the table. A wide grin split his face. "So she beat you again, huh, Michael?" Joanna's ability to beat Michael at Monopoly had become the family joke.

Michael growled something under his breath about upstart, insolent children that made both Joanna and Patrick laugh.

Patrick was nearly a mirror image of his older brothers, but there was something a bit more youthful and playful about him. He didn't have Michael's serious sense of responsibility, nor did he possess Danny's never-ending sense of calm. He also had a wicked set of dimples on either side of his mouth that made him, if possible, even more appealing.

As the youngest, Patrick had been in his older brother's shadow his whole life. He was as tall as Michael, but much more hotheaded and impulsive than Danny, earning his own rather stellar reputation in the neighborhood.

Patrick had struggled to carve a niche for himself, one his older brothers hadn't already traversed, leading to a whole host of interesting…adventures as Maeve so delicately put it. Rather than try to outshine his brothers, Patrick had finally merely carved his own separate place in the world.

"Hey, Joanna. I just came up to tell you I'm free Monday, so after your doctor's appointment I thought we'd go for lunch. There's this great new tapas joint that opened—"

"Topless?" Michael stood abruptly, a scowl deeply etched in his brow. His eyes had an unmistakable feral gleam. "Are you out of your mind, Patrick?" His voice boomed around the room. "You can't take Joanna to a topless bar for lunch."

Patrick shook his head, then dropped a friendly arm around his big brother's shoulder. "Down, tiger. I didn't say *topless,* I said *tapas.*" Still grinning, Patrick tightened his arm around Michael's neck, speaking close to his face. "You know—a Spanish restaurant with small portions meant to share. Garlic potato salad. Filet stuffed with blue cheese. Pasta with Spanish rice and beans? Are you getting my drift here, bro?"

Michael let out a sigh of relief. "Got it," he said, glancing at Joanna sheepishly. He frowned again. "But I don't think she should be eating all that spicy food. It's probably not good for her or the baby."

Joanna gave Michael a poke. "Yes, *Dad,*" she teased, scowling and crossing her arms over her breasts. "I'm old enough to know what I can eat and where I can go." She grinned at Patrick. "And just for your information, I think it might be interesting to go to a topless joint for lunch." The idea of aggravating Michael about this had immense appeal. "It might be fun."

"Don't start," Michael warned. "I'm worried enough here. I don't need anything else to worry about." He turned to his brother. "And you're no help."

Amused, Patrick shrugged. "I wasn't trying to be." He grabbed a handful of popcorn, popped it into his mouth, then scowled. "Yuk." He grabbed the bowl, inspected, then sniffed it. "Are you sure this is popcorn? It tastes like those little plastic things they use for packing."

Laughing, Joanna shook her head. "Your brother's idea of healthy food."

"It's fat-free, salt-free, and good for Joanna," Michael interjected, crossing his arms across his chest defensively.

"Well, there's a reason to eat it," Patrick said dryly, setting the bowl back down on the table. "You guys going for your walk?" Patrick glanced at the window. "It's still teeming out there." He glanced back at Michael, his eyes glinting in amusement. "Better be careful, Michael, with the way the wind's blowing, Joanna might, uh, get blown into Lake Michigan. I'd keep a tight grip on her if I were you." A full-blown smile broke loose and Michael growled again.

"Patrick, don't you have someplace you have to be?" He'd be grateful to have his brother anywhere but *here* right now. His entire family had embraced Joanna from the moment she'd moved in. Both Danny and Patrick treated her in the same loving, teasing manner they'd always treated Katie. In spite of his own occasional aggravation at his brother's teasing because he was, he had to admit, at times overprotective of Joanna, he loved his family for making her feel so welcome and so at home.

And they'd taken to teasing him about his protective, or as his mother, Da and his brothers asserted, overprotective attitude. But as he so clearly pointed out, he'd never taken care of a pregnant lady before. He was just being…careful and responsible.

Propping his shoulder against the wall, Patrick shook his head. "Nope. I'm off duty and done for the night." He crossed his arms across his chest. "I don't have a thing to do except aggravate you."

"Wonderful," Michael growled.

"Patrick." Deciding to intervene before there was bloodshed, Joanna pressed a hand to her back, then smoothed down her maternity top. "Are you sure this is okay? About Monday and the doctor?" Her brows drew together. "I don't want you to go to any trouble on my account."

It was still hard not to feel like a bother. Not that the Sullivans had made her feel anything less than welcome. It was her own feelings that were the problem, not theirs.

The Sullivans had been wonderful to her. Each and every one of them. They'd accepted her into their home and their hearts, treating her like one of the family. It had been an incredible experience, one she knew she would cherish and never forget. Not one single moment of it.

Michael had given her a precious gift, a glimpse of something she'd never known, and she would forever be grateful to him.

"No trouble. I told you that." Patrick reached out and ruffled her hair with one hand, while grabbing another handful of popcorn with the other. "Danny got to take you last week. I want a turn. Besides, I've got the day off." He wiggled his brows. "I thought maybe after lunch, we'd sneak into a movie." He glanced at Michael. "That is if it's all right with your jailer." Patrick grinned at the expression on Michael's face.

"Jailer?" Clearly affronted, Michael gave his brother a look that would have felled anyone else on the spot. "And never mind *sneaking* into a movie, Patrick. Joanna's in no condition to be sneaking anywhere."

"That was a figure of speech, bro," Patrick said with an amused shake of his head. He and Joanna exchanged glances. "I fully intend to pay. I'm an officer of the law, remember?"

"Just make sure *you* remember," Michael growled. "Now go aggravate someone else, bro, Joanna's tired."

"Hey, if Joanna's going to bed, why don't you come down to the pub and have a beer with me? Danny should be off duty in an hour or so."

Concerned, Michael shook his head. "No, I don't—"

"Michael." Joanna smiled. "That's a great idea. You haven't been out since I moved in. Go have a beer with your brothers. I'll be fine," she promised, her smile widening.

He dragged a hand through his hair. "I don't know."

"Michael." She sighed. "You can't stand guard over me twenty-four hours a day until I have this baby. I'm tired and will be sleeping anyway." She gave him a helpful push in the back. "It will be good for you to get out of here for a change."

"You're sure?"

"Positive." She looked at Patrick for help. It had amazed her how quick the bond between her and the Sullivans had formed. With just a look, or a word, it seemed as if she was able to communicate with any of them on some level.

Patrick nodded, still munching the offensive popcorn. He hooked an arm around his brother's shoulder and guided him toward the door before he could protest. "Come on, it'll do you good." He glanced over his shoulder and winked. "Don't forget about Monday."

"I won't. I'll be ready."

"Lock the door," Michael cautioned as Patrick practically dragged him through it.

"Michael, your entire family is—"

"The door, Joanna." He came to a stop and waited. Shaking her head, she did as she was told, shutting the door softly, then locking it with a decided click. With a smile and a yawn, she headed toward her bedroom, listening to the quiet sound of the rain patter on the roof.

Something woke him up.

Michael bolted upright in bed, automatically grabbing his jeans off the chair. It was still raining, and the house was dark. Dragging his jeans on, he listened, his ears tuned to any sound. Then he heard it.

Joanna.

Barefoot, with only his jeans on, he bolted out the door. Her bedroom door was closed, but the light was on. His pulse sped up.

"Joanna?" Quietly he knocked on the door. He heard a moan, and realized that's what woke him. She had been moaning. He didn't wait for her to answer, but merely opened the door and barged in.

She was sitting up in bed, rubbing her belly. Her long hair was sleep-tousled, and her face had a hint of strain he'd never seen before. He was at her side in an instant.

"What?" he'd demanded. "Is it the baby?" Panic had seized him in spite of the preparations and plans they'd made.

"No," she'd told him. "Just Braxton-Hicks." She tried not to stare at his bare chest. He was barefoot, with his jeans carelessly dragged over his hips. Zipped but not snapped. She was absolutely certain he'd never looked as devastating. Quickly she averted her eyes and channeled her thoughts.

"Braxton who?" He shook his head, aware that she was still wincing and holding her stomach. "Who's Braxton…whatever?" He sat on the side of the bed, needing something solid beneath him.

"It's not a who, Michael, but a what." She took a slow, deep breath as Dr. Summers had instructed. "They're contractions." She held out a hand to stop him as he nearly bolted from the room, certain this was it. "Relax, Michael. They're not the real thing. They're sort of like…practice contractions." She grinned at the look on his face. "Think of it as a dress rehearsal."

"I see," he said, not seeing anything of the kind. "But why?" He dragged a hand through his tousled hair. "I mean, what's the point?"

"It's to prepare my body for actual labor and delivery."

"Do they hurt?" He wasn't certain he was going to be able to handle just sitting by and watching her in pain.

"A little," she admitted, taking quick puffs of breath. She rubbed her belly again. "Here. Feel." She reached for his hand. Hesitantly he laid it over her stomach and waited. A few moments later he felt it. It was almost as strong as the day he'd felt the baby move for the first time. Her stomach hardened for a few seconds, then relaxed.

"Wow," he whispered, awed again at how much the female body went through to bear children. He shook his head, yanking his hand back. "How long has this been going on?"

"About an hour."

"An hour?" He studied her face. Underneath the calm, he could see a hint of fear in her eyes. It wrapped around his heart. He took her hand, cradling it in his, wanting to comfort. "Why didn't you wake me up?" He stroked a tumbled length of hair off her face, wondering why she'd just sat here alone and in pain. Then he remembered, this was Joanna. She wouldn't think to do anything else. Calling for him, or asking for help or company probably never entered her mind.

She smiled. "Why wake you up? There's nothing you or anyone else can do. Dr. Summers said they would probably start happening the closer I got to my delivery date." She shrugged. "There didn't seem any point in disturbing your sleep as well."

"It can't be much fun sitting all alone, in pain." He studied her face. "You can't tell me that it's not a little frightening?"

In all these months, no matter what she'd gone through she'd never once uttered a complaint about what was happening to her poor body. He had to admit he found her behavior not just courageous, but admirable.

"Just…a little," she admitted, and he knew it cost her. Admitting she needed something was still very, very difficult for her.

"You should have woken me up," he admonished gently. "Is this why your back's been bothering you so much the past few days?"

She nodded. "Probably." Having Michael sitting on her bed, barely dressed, holding her hand, was making her incredibly nervous and far too aware of him. She felt silly considering the circumstances.

"Can I get you something?"

She licked her lips and forced a smile. "Maybe a little something to drink, Michael."

"I'll be right back." He headed toward the kitchen and returned with an ice-cold can of Squirt and a glass. Pouring as he came into the room, he handed it to her, watching as she drank.

"How long do you think these things will last?" He took the empty glass from her and set it on the nightstand.

"I'm not sure, Michael." She shrugged. "A few more minutes or a few more hours. There's no way to tell."

"Hours?" He was absolutely certain he didn't like that idea. "Would it help if I rubbed your back?"

She smiled. Having Michael rub her back when she was uncomfortable was an incomparable luxury.

"It might."

"Move over." He pulled the comforter down, and slid in beside her. Taking her by the shoulders, he turned her away from him, then gently began to massage her back, starting at her shoulders. "God, you're as tight as a drum." She was coiled in tension. "Here, let's try this."

He leaned against the headboard, and stretched his long legs out, helping her to sit between them. Gently he pulled her back until she was leaning against him. Slowly he massaged her shoulders, kneading the tense muscles.

With a sigh, Joanna relaxed against him. "That feels so wonderful," she murmured, very grateful Michael was here. She *had* been a bit frightened. She hadn't told Michael, but the Braxton-Hicks contractions had been coming more and more frequently. She knew to expect them, but what she didn't know was if it was normal for them to come so often. She made a mental note to ask the doctor about it Monday.

"Just relax, hon," he whispered into her ear. His soft, warm breath fanned over her and sent a wicked shiver through her. The warmth of his body seeped into hers, calming and soothing. His chest was bare. Hard and strong, it seemed like a stable haven to rest against.

"Just try to relax."

Michael's gentle, clever hands worked the sore muscles of her back until she was nearly purring. As she relaxed, the contractions seemed to ease. She was so tired. Waking up every night in the middle of the night was wreaking havoc on her sleep patterns. It was a rare night when she got more than two or three hours of uninterrupted sleep. It left her chronically fatigued, which only made her feel more uncomfortable.

"*Ahhh,* that feels so good, Michael," she whispered, feeling incredibly drowsy.

"Feeling better?" His deep voice was whisper-soft. He reached out and tugged the comforter up, covering them both. From the sound of her voice he could tell she was relaxing and getting sleepy. "How are the contractions?"

She sighed dreamily. "Almost gone, I think." He was so warm and soft, and she was so tired. She wanted to just curl up and snuggle in his arms.

"Joanna?"

"Hmm?"

"Why don't you try to get some sleep?" As if he'd heard her thoughts, he wrapped both his arms around her and cradled her close against him. "Lean your head back against me." Too tired to protest, she did, letting her head fall back against his shoulder. "Stretch out your legs, hon, and get comfortable."

"Michael—"

"Shh, I'm here. I'm not going anywhere. Just relax and go to sleep." He pressed a kiss to her cheek, making her smile sleepily. Her eyes drooped and she snuggled closer to him, enjoying the feeling of being held by him far too much to protest.

"Michael?"

"What, hon?" he whispered, reaching out to snap out the light.

She turned slightly, until her whole body was cradled against the entire length of him. In spite of the differences in their sizes they seemed to fit together perfectly.

"Thank you," she murmured, laying her hands on his bare chest, and then her face on her hands.

Before he could respond, she was asleep. He watched

her for a moment, feeling something so strong, so primal in his gut, in his heart, it scared the hell out of him.

Smiling at how beautiful, how peaceful she looked, he leaned down and gently brushed his lips across hers in a feather kiss. He couldn't resist. Satisfied she was safe, asleep, and no longer in pain, Michael sighed deeply, then leaned his head back, and went to sleep, feeling more content than he could ever remember.

Chapter Eight

"Da, I've got fifty bucks that says it's going to be a boy." Confident, Danny winked at Joanna as he threw a fifty-dollar bill into the middle of his mother's huge dining-room table where the entire family had gathered for Sunday dinner.

Sunday dinner together was a family tradition. It was the one day of the week when the pub remained closed, giving everyone time to spend with their family.

In the past month, winter had finally relinquished its stubborn hold. As the month of April slipped into May, spring began peeking around the corner. The dark, dismal rains of April had given way to the first warm, sunny days of May. Flowers began to bud and bloom and children looked forward to the end of school.

"Fifty! Posh!" Da said with a sad shake of his head. "What do you know about babies, Danny boy?" he demanded, his white brows furrowed. "Besides how to make one?"

Everyone laughed good-naturedly as Da turned his experienced eye on Joanna, studying her carefully.

The Sullivans had not only taken her into their home and their hearts, but her unborn child as well. She wasn't quite sure when the baby became community Sullivan property, she realized suddenly, thrilled beyond belief. Probably sometime in the past six weeks since she'd moved in.

Da was still studying her, his brows furrowed in concentration. "Would you mind standing up, lass?" he said with a smile, gentling his voice with her. He held out his hand and helped her up, turning her this way and that, mumbling something under his breath.

"You've grown a bit in the past month and a half," he admitted with a gleeful smile, obviously pleased. He nodded his head. "Aye, it might be a boy," he conceded finally, glancing at his upstart grandson, Danny, "but I doubt she'll go the distance." With the customary twinkle in his eye, he looked up at Joanna. "When's the doctor predicting the blessing will arrive?"

Joanna couldn't help but smile. Since she'd come to live with Michael, she'd gotten quite accustomed to Da's quaint way of speaking. Even though he'd been in this country for almost sixty years, he still clung to bits and pieces of the language of his birth, making for a charming, if occasionally confusing, vocabulary.

"The doctor says my due date is June 15, give or take a day or two." She laid a hand on her belly. "Only about six more weeks."

"Six weeks you say?" Da said, considering. Still frowning, he continued to appraise her. "Turn a bit to the right, lass." She did as he instructed, exchanging an amused glance with Michael, who was quietly sipping his coffee, staying out of the family fray.

Joanna stood very still, aware that everyone's eyes were on her. She glanced around the table, feeling a surge of warmth and happiness. Danny, Patrick and Katie were sitting on one side, while she, Michael and his mother were seated on the other side. Da still commanded the head of the table, but she was pleased that from the moment she'd arrived, Da had insisted she sit next to him, claiming he was sick and tired of looking only at the male faces of his grandsons. She knew it was his way of making her feel comfortable, and she couldn't help but love him for it.

"Now the other way, lass," Da instructed, still intently studying her with a frown. Finally he shook his head. "I watched Maeve carry three boys, and my own lovely girl—may she rest in peace—carry six, and I'll put my money on a boy, but I don't believe the lass will go the distance. No sirree."

He counted the weeks on his finger, looking up at her in surprise. "Nay, she'll never last another six weeks." He shook his white head again. "Not the way the gal is carrying." He glanced at his grandson Danny. "I'll take your fifty bet, son, agreeing she'll deliver a boy, but I'll up you fifty more that says she doesn't go the distance."

Grinning, Da released Joanna's hand to reach for his breast pocket wallet, carefully extracting one hundred dollars in crisp bills, which promptly was added to the growing pile in the middle of the table.

"So it's a boy you're saying," Maeve said, coming back into the dining room with a fresh pot of coffee. She glanced at Michael with a smile, aware that his eyes never were far from Joanna. "And what is it you say, son?" Maeve began pouring coffee all around, keeping an eye on her eldest son.

Michael laughed, reaching out his hand to help Joanna to her seat. "Well, I hate to admit it but I think I have the inside track." He winked at her, before glancing around the table. "Da, Danny, my money's on a girl."

"A girl!" Patrick exclaimed with a shake of his head. "That's a bet you're going to lose, big brother." He sipped his coffee, grinning at Joanna over the rim. "Sullivan genes only run to males, Joanna," he explained to her. "Have you forgotten, Michael, there hasn't been a female born to a Sullivan in three generations."

For a moment, there was an awkward, uncomfortable silence, then laughter erupted around the room. Patrick glanced around the table in confusion.

"What? What did I say?"

Joanna's gaze flew to Michael's and for a moment, she felt a wave of embarrassment. Then she saw the amusement on Michael's face and relaxed, feeling a grin sneak up on her. She wondered if Patrick even realized the implications of what he'd said.

Laying his hand over hers under the table, Michael shook his head, reaching across the table with his other hand to whack Patrick in the head.

"You idiot, did you forget this kid's not a Sullivan?"

Feeling sheepish, Patrick glanced around the table, then at Joanna. "Jeez, sorry, guess I did forget."

Watching them now, she couldn't help but smile. They were loud, boisterous, and yet so totally loving it was hard not to be impressed or drawn into the circle of warmth. It was clear that the Sullivans stuck together through thick and thin. She envied them their closeness, their charm and their history. They were a family in the truest sense of the word.

"We can fix that, can't we, Joanna?" Patrick winked at her.

She shifted her weight, suddenly feeling an odd sort of pressure that was strangely uncomfortable. She shifted again, trying to find some relief. Determined not to let on to anyone the discomfort she was feeling, she forced a smile, realizing Patrick was trying to draw her into the fray, treating her the same way he'd treat Katie or his brothers. It pleased her.

"We can?" she asked with a lift of her brow, trying to ignore the twinge of a contraction that fluttered through her. It was probably just another Braxton-Hicks. She'd been having them off and on for the past four weeks.

"Are you proposing, Patrick?" she asked, grinning at Michael. He gave her hand an approving squeeze under the table and she tried not to let on that she was feeling some discomfort. Michael had a tendency to panic at the thought of her being in any kind of pain.

Patrick paled as everyone laughed. He darted a glance at his older brother Michael, who was enjoying the joke as much as everyone.

"Proposing?" Patrick fairly croaked the word out, shaking his head in dismay. He swallowed hard. "Jeez, Joanna, I was thinking more along the lines of adopting you."

Everyone groaned.

"Yeah." Katie chimed in with a grin. "Patrick's far too committed to the single life to ever get married."

"Right again," he said with a smile. "Why would I want to saddle myself with one woman, when the whole world is filled with them?"

"Said just like a man," Katie said, tossing her crumpled napkin at him. "And like your brother." No one had to ask which brother she was referring to. Danny merely gave her a sidelong glance and for a moment tension crackled between them. Once best friends, a falling-out had left them barely speaking to each other. A fact that annoyed and angered Maeve.

"I still say it's a girl." Michael winked at Joanna, knowing he was trusting her mother's intuition. He looked at her carefully. She looked a little pale to him.

"Put your money where your mouth is, boy," Da said with a smile. He picked up his coffee, sipped, made a face at how weak it was, then set his cup down again.

"You got it." Leaning back in his chair, Michael dug into his pants, extracting some crumpled bills, which he threw into the pile. "My money—one hundred bucks says it's a girl."

"What about going the distance, son?" Da asked, one brow raised. "Will the lass go the distance?"

"Doesn't matter," Michael said, not wanting to think about how close she was to delivering. Since she had moved in with him, it seemed as if time was going in triple-time.

He knew that once the baby was born he'd have a hard time convincing her to stay with him, knowing she'd want to go back to her own home, and her own life. And her independence.

He had no idea how he was going to cope with reality when it came. The thought of her and the baby all alone…he couldn't even bear it. Like everything else, he pushed the thought away. Buried it. He'd deal with it when the time came.

He grinned at his grandfather. "Going the distance or not, my money's on a girl. Plain and simple."

"That's a bet you'll lose." Patrick grinned, pushing his cup away. "I'm putting my money on a boy, and I think she *will* go the distance." He threw his money into the pile, making Maeve shake her head.

"Betting good money on Joanna like she was a race-horse," she said, setting the coffeepot down in the middle of the table. "Shame on you." Her glance took in her entire family. "If your father were here—"

"If Jock were here, Maeve," Da interrupted, "he'd be the first one with his money out. Has he been gone so long you've forgotten how he dearly loved a spirited bet?"

Maeve laughed. "You're right, Da. He'd have loved it." She glanced at Joanna affectionately. "He would have loved you, too, dear." Her gaze shifted to Da, one brow raised in reproach. "But Jock would also be betting and praying for a healthy baby, no matter the gender."

"Aye," Da said with a sigh, properly reprimanded. "You're right again, as always, Maeve." He glanced around the table. "It goes without saying we want the babe to be strong and healthy."

"Not to mention on time." Danny reached for the pile of money, scooping it close to him. "Let's see what we've got here. Brat," he said to Katie, "get a pad and keep score." Katie went to retrieve a notepad while Danny began to count.

"I'm definitely going to clean up," Michael whispered to Joanna.

She lifted a brow at him, ignoring another contraction. "Don't you mean *we?*" She grinned at Maeve who was watching them intently. "Seems to me you've got insider information so the least you can do is…share."

Absently she rubbed her tummy, hoping the contractions would subside soon. She didn't have that much energy these days, and they had a tendency to wear her out.

With a smile, Maeve nodded in approval. "That's what I like, a woman who can keep my son in line."

"Hey, it's two against one," Michael complained with a grin. "Not fair."

"Who ever told you life was fair?" Da asked with a grin, giving Joanna a wink. "When there's a lass involved, life's never fair. We just make do the best we can." Shaking his head in dismay, Da sipped his coffee. "Although why they've been called the fairer sex has always been a puzzle to me."

"All right." Danny separated the money into neat piles of tens, twenties and fifties. "There's three hundred and fifty in the pot. Fifty from me. A hundred from Da, Michael and Patrick. Michael's money's on a girl. Da's is on a boy, but with a stipulation that Joanna doesn't go the distance. Patrick's money's on a boy, and a stipulation that Joanna does go the distance. Mine's just a straight bet of a boy, no matter when she delivers." He glanced at Katie. "Got it, brat?"

"Got it." Seemingly annoyed at his use of her childhood nickname, she ripped off the sheet of paper and slid it across the table to him.

He picked it and the money up and handed it to his mother. "Here, you're a neutral bystander, and you look like a trustworthy individual, you hold the bounty."

"Indeed I will," Maeve said, scooping the money and

the note into her apron pocket. She rose. "If no one's wanting anything else, I'll start clearing the table, then."

"I'll help," Joanna offered, starting to get up.

"No!" The entire table caroled in unison. Michael pressed a hand to her shoulder, making her sit right back down. She was hoping that maybe a bit of walking might stop the Braxton-Hicks.

"You need to be off your feet," Maeve said, stacking dirty plates. "Not carrying dishes in and out of the kitchen." Maeve glanced at her son. "Michael, why don't you and Joanna go for a ride." She glanced toward the window. The sun was shining brilliantly, the breeze warm enough to leave the windows open, giving a breath of air after the stuffiness of winter. "It's a beautiful day. A drive might relax her."

Michael glanced at his watch, then pushed his chair out, standing up. "Good idea, Ma." He pulled Joanna's chair out and helped her up. He glanced at his watch again. "We'll be back around six," he said pointedly, looking at his mother.

She nodded, pleased. "Six it is, then."

"Are you sure I can't help, Maeve?" Joanna rubbed her stomach again as another contraction came, then peaked.

"Positive," she replied with a grin. "Go enjoy the day."

Joanna went up to get a sweater while Michael got the car. Even though it was warm, or at least warmer than it had been, she didn't want to get chilled. She was just pulling her sweater on when Michael pulled the car around.

He got out to open the door and help her in, catching a brief scent of her perfume. He would always associate that scent with Joanna. It was undeniably hers. He hadn't realized how much her scent, her presence would play havoc with his feelings.

Since the night she'd moved in, he'd deliberately controlled any emotion that surfaced. It was beginning to become a strain, wrecking his nights, and intruding on his sleep. But he'd told her she could trust him, depend on him, and he was as good as his word.

"Any particular place you'd like to go today?" he asked as he climbed behind the wheel. She shook her head feeling full and drowsy as she so often did now after a meal.

"No place special." She smiled dreamily at him as she leaned her head against the headrest. She loved going for rides with Michael. "Surprise me."

With the soft wind blowing through her hair, she tried to relax. The contractions apparently were here for a while, so she might as well just go with the flow. There was little else she could do until they stopped. She'd just try to relax and concentrate on the ride.

She and Michael frequently went for drives now, particularly at night when she had trouble sleeping. The baby was in such a position it was difficult for her to get comfortable, and the baby was so active, at times she felt as if her ribs were bruised. She was uncomfortable most of the time now. Each day seeming to bring another minor ache, pain or worry. She couldn't imagine how other women went through this eight or nine times, not without worrying themselves to death.

"Don't forget, we start childbirth classes this week," she reminded him, watching his profile. Absently she rubbed her stomach again.

"How could I forget?" Michael asked, heading out of the neighborhood. He thought he'd jump on the expressway and head to the suburbs for a while as a change of pace. "You're sure about this? You're sure you want me as your coach and not my ma or Katie?"

She knew he was nervous about it, but in spite of his nerves, he'd offered, not waiting for her to ask and she'd loved him for it.

"Michael." She laid a hand on his arm. "You've been through my entire pregnancy with me. There isn't anyone else I'd rather have there." She gave his arm a reassuring squeeze. "You belong there. But if you don't—"

"No, no, no," he said firmly. "I want to be there, that's why I offered." He swallowed, hoping he had the strength, never mind the courage to go through with this coaching thing. "I'm honored, it's just I'm still not sure—"

"Michael," she said with a laugh. "You'll do fine. It's a perfectly natural experience, nothing to worry about." She found it amusing that this big, tough lieutenant could be awed and intimidated at the prospect of childbirth.

"Still," he said as he swung the car onto the expressway. "I just don't want to disappoint you."

It was the last thing he'd ever want to do. But he had no idea how he'd handle the idea, never mind the actuality of Joanna being in pain.

Rationally, in his head, he understood the childbirth process, but it was his heart that was giving him problems. How he was going to stand there, and be a help to her while she was in pain without going nuts or killing someone was going to be a challenge.

He glanced at her, grateful she was relaxing. "Are you up for some of Milano's Italian ice?" It was a forty-five minute ride each way, but the drive was worth it to make her happy. Italian ice was something she could eat without worrying about salt or calories since it was basically just flavored ice. On Sundays, after dinner, they frequently drove out to Milano's.

Pleased and surprised, she laughed. "Always. I'd love some Italian ice." Feeling a little tired, she closed her eyes and let the gentle motion of the car lull her.

Michael watched her. With her eyes closed, and her lips slightly parted, he was certain she'd never looked more beautiful. She worried about the weight she'd put on the past few weeks. Almost seven pounds, but Dr. Summers had explained that the further along in her pregnancy, the more weight she'd gain and the more water she'd retain. It was a necessary hazard.

He'd been watching her like a hawk, making sure she did everything she was supposed to do. Since the night he'd awakened to find her having those Braxton-Hicks contractions, he'd taken to sleeping on the floor of her bedroom, so he'd be there in case she woke or needed anything. More nights than not, she woke up, and invariably he ended up climbing into bed with her, and rubbing her back or her shoulders until she fell asleep in his arms.

He hated to admit it felt wonderful to hold her all night. To have her close, and feel her warmth. More importantly, in his mind, it was the final sign that she'd grown to trust him, to depend on him as he'd asked. At least for a little while and nothing could have made him happier.

As he shot off the expressway and headed toward Milano's he gently touched her shoulder to wake her. "Joanna?"

"Michael," she murmured, still half-asleep and more relaxed than she'd been in days.

"Yeah." He grinned, liking the sexy, sultry way she said his name. "We're almost at Milano's, hon."

She sat up, rubbing her eyes and pushing her hair back as he pulled into the parking lot. Another contraction gripped her, and she took a long, deep breath until it was over. She didn't dare rub her stomach to ease it, knowing Michael would probably panic as he did so often these days when he thought anything was wrong with her.

"I look a mess," she complained, pulling down the visor to examine herself.

"You look beautiful," he assured her, snapping the visor back into place. His words made her smile.

"Thank you, Michael, but I know what I look like." She laughed as he helped her out of the car. "A blond blimp."

He took her hand as they started toward the ice-cream parlor. "Perhaps, but you're still the most beautiful blond blimp I've ever seen." He leaned down and kissed her nose, making her laugh.

"How come I never knew what an accomplished liar

you are?'' she asked as he opened the door and led her to a booth in the back of the parlor.

''Me?'' He shrugged his shoulders. ''Would I ever lie to you?'' His words echoed hollowly in his mind as a flash of guilt rolled over him. He'd lied to her, been lying to her for the almost seven months since the day of Brian's death.

He'd hoped to find the right time to tell her, to explain about what had gone down that day. But the opportunity hadn't really presented itself, not to mention the fact that he hadn't quite found his courage, either. Now, he knew that by telling her the truth, after what they'd been through together, he would risk the fragile bond of trust she'd given to him. The thought scared the hell out of him. It wasn't something he was certain he could face. At least not yet.

As Joanna pushed three scoops of Italian ice around, trying to make it look as if she'd eaten it, the contractions seemed to be continuing, zapping her appetite. She and Michael talked and laughed about everything and nothing, including the fact that the irrepressible Pearl had once again entered the Sullivans' life, but this time it was Danny she was after, much to Danny's chagrin.

It was about five-thirty when they exited the ice-cream parlor, and the sky had turned to a burnished orange in preparation for nightfall. The air smelled warm and sweet, a promise of summer to come.

Michael glanced at his watch as they headed toward the car, remembering his promise to get Joanna back by six.

Traffic was light, and they made the trip back home in less than forty-five minutes. Rather than pulling into the garage since it was still so early, Michael pulled in front of the pub.

''Michael?'' Joanna said with a frown. ''I thought the pub was closed on Sunday.''

''It is,'' he said as he parked, and snapped off the ignition.

''Then why are there lights on in there?'' Feeling apprehensive, she glanced at him, wondering why he didn't appear too concerned.

"Let's go find out." He helped her from the car, grabbing the sweater she'd discarded in deference to the warmth. Holding her arm, he led her to the front door, where he fumbled with his keys. Finally finding the right one, he swung the door open, taking her hand and pulling her in behind him.

For a moment Joanna froze, stunned, wondering what was going on as she stared at a sea of familiar faces gathered in the pub. She glanced up at Michael, noted he was grinning like the cat who had swallowed a canary.

"Michael?" Clutching his hand tighter, she glanced from the sea of smiling faces, back to Michael. Still stunned, and not sure what was going on, time seemed to move in slow motion. Her voice, her eyes held a question, just as the room erupted in shouts and laughter.

"Surprise!" The room seemed to carol the word in unison, making her blink. Maeve stepped forward and took her hands. "Come on in, Joanna." She gave her son a look. "I was heartily afraid my son was going to make you miss your own baby shower."

Chapter Nine

Touched beyond measure, tears filled Joanna's eyes as Maeve stepped up to hug her. "I'm not just surprised, I'm shocked," she blubbered, swiping at her eyes. "How? When?" Laughing, she shook her head, drew back, then glanced at Michael, feeling a surge of emotion so strong it rocked her. Dear Michael. "And you," she said, giving him a whack on the arm. "Why didn't you tell me?"

"And risk the wrath of my mother?" Grinning in delight, he shook his head. It made him happy to see her so happy. "Nope. Not me. I'm no fool."

"Come say hello to everyone," Maeve said, taking her hand. She turned toward her son. "And you…go…do something. We'll call you if we need you."

Michael headed out to park his car in the garage, pleased that he'd been able to keep this secret from Joanna, but then again, he thought sadly, he'd gotten very good at keeping things from her.

When his mother first told him about the shower, he was more pleased than he could say, knowing how much it would mean to Joanna. He headed out the door, to park his car and go play cards with his brothers.

"I'm just so stunned," Joanna said, her eyes drifting to Michael's retreating figure. Wistfully she watched him, wishing he could have stayed, but knew he probably wouldn't relish the idea of sitting among a group of women who would be *oohing* and *ahhing* over baby paraphernalia.

Wiping her eyes, she let Maeve lead her around the room. It looked as if everyone in the neighborhood had shown up. Spotting Mrs. O'Bannion, more tears filled her eyes and she hugged the older woman tightly. "Mrs. O'Bannion, I've missed you."

"I've missed you, too." Mrs. O'Bannion laughed, patting Joanna's belly. "You've gotten so big," she commented, always tactful. "Pretty soon, huh?"

"Not soon enough," she said with a laugh as Maeve continued to lead her around the room to greet her guests. After she'd said hello to everyone, Joanna glanced around the pub for the first time, impressed. "Maeve, when on earth did you have the time to do all of this?"

Every inch of the pub had been decorated with pink and blue streamers and balloons. In the center of the room was a table draped in pink and blue, atop it a pile of presents.

Maeve grinned, leading Joanna to an empty chair in the center of the room. "I can't take credit for the decorations, dear. The boys did it. Last night after the pub closed, and you were asleep, they came down and set everything up." She shrugged, glancing at the bulging buffet tables. "I cooked a little bit every day just so you wouldn't notice."

Overcome with love, Joanna hugged Maeve again. "Thank you," she whispered. "Thank you so much." Another precious gift. One she'd never expected. One she would always treasure.

"Sit. Sit," Maeve ordered with a wave of her hand. "We'll open presents and then eat."

Joanna sat, grateful to be off her feet. The contractions

continued and she was beginning to get a bit nervous about them. She wasn't sure Braxton-Hicks contractions were supposed to last this long, or grow in intensity. As uncomfortable as she was, she didn't want to do anything to spoil the party, not after Maeve and everyone else had gone to so much trouble.

"The first present, dear, is from me." Maeve glanced at Da who stood guard over the bar, ladling nonalcoholic punch into glasses from the big bowl sitting on the bar. With a grin, he wheeled a beautiful antique cradle topped with pink and blue bows toward Joanna. Her breath caught at the beauty of it.

"This cradle was Jock's," Maeve said softly, as Da wheeled it close enough to Joanna to see.

"Made of sturdy Irish wood," Da pronounced proudly, patting the cradle as if testing its strength.

"It was carved by hand with love," Maeve explained softly, as her eyes misted with memories. Reverently she ran a hand over the edge of the cradle, as if the touch brought a sense of peace.

"It's been passed down from generation to generation. It's been said that the first Sullivan male carved this cradle for his ladylove. T'was to be a gift for their wedding day. But then he learned she could never be his since she was pledged to another." Shaking her head, Maeve laughed suddenly. "Like a true Sullivan, it was said in a fit of anger, he was going to toss this fine piece into the sea. But alas, a Sullivan in love is a force to be reckoned with, and somehow, both he, his ladylove and their wee ones ended up together, and made fine use of the cradle they did. It's been in the family ever since. A precious heirloom of memories, passed down." Lost in memories, Maeve laid a gentle hand on the cradle to set it rocking.

"I used it for my own boys when they were babes." With a smile, Maeve glanced at Katie, then back at Joanna. "I had hoped to have a daughter of my own to pass it on to." She took Joanna's hand, and reached for Katie's. The three women, hands entwined, stood together.

"God blessed me with two daughters," Maeve said softly, her eyes swimming with tears as she looked at the two young women who had claimed her heart. "Aye, perhaps not by birth, but by love." She touched Joanna's cheek. "I would be honored if you'd use it for your wee one." She kissed her. "Honored, indeed."

"Oh, Maeve." Overcome by emotion, Joanna hugged Maeve. Nothing in her life had ever meant more to her. Or ever touched her more. Emotions swamped, then swarmed over her. Tears spilled from her eyes as she hugged Maeve tight.

"I've never had a mother," she whispered. "Never knew what a mother's love was like." She drew back and looked at Maeve. "I do now." Smiling through her tears, she kissed Maeve's cheek, then hugged her again. "Thank you." She hugged her tighter. "Thank you for everything."

Hugging her back, Maeve felt Joanna stiffen. It set off an alarm bell. Drawing back, Maeve searched her face carefully, noting she had paled and there was a hint of pain mixed with panic in her eyes. This wasn't emotions, but something far more.

"What is it?" she asked in a quiet, sure way.

"I'm not sure," Joanna whispered. She sat down in the chair, feeling shaky. "I've been having Braxton-Hicks contractions all day, or at least I thought they were Braxton-Hicks." Her breath caught and she grabbed her stomach as another contraction hit. This one harder, and stronger, strong enough to make her breath catch. "But I think my water is leaking." She wasn't going to panic. She wasn't. She was probably mistaken. Perhaps something else was going on. It was too early for the baby. Far too early. She took a deep breath to stay calm, wishing Michael was here.

"How far apart are the contractions?" Maeve asked, her voice calm, face concerned.

Joanna winced again, shifting her weight as another one hit. "I'm not sure, I haven't timed them, but they've been pretty steady since right before we sat down to dinner."

Maeve glanced at her watch. "That was almost six hours ago." She stood up, frowning. "Da," she called. "Go up and get the boys."

"What's the trouble…" Da's voice trailed off at the look on Maeve and Joanna's faces. "I'll step to it, Maeve." Da raced out the back door and up the stairs, yelling for his grandsons, who were seated at the dining-room table engaged in a heated game of poker.

"Da." Michael was on his feet in a flash. "What is it?"

"It's Joanna." Da shook his head. "Something's wrong, Mikey. You'd best come."

Michael pushed past his brothers and took the stairs down three at a time. Ignoring the roomful of women, he headed straight for Joanna and his mother, with Patrick, Danny and Da right on his heels.

"What's wrong?" His eyes went from his mother to Joanna. Panic rolled over him making his knees weak. His pulse seemed to stutter in fear.

"Michael, I think you should take Joanna to the hospital to have Dr. Summers check her out." Maeve patted her hand trying to be reassuring. "It's probably nothing, a false alarm, but I'd feel better if she was checked out."

Fear caught him in its fiery grip. Michael's heart was pounding so hard, he was absolutely certain it was going to pound right through his chest.

"Should I call an ambulance?" Danny asked, poking his head closer.

"No," Maeve said with a shake of her head. "It will take too long for it to get here. Michael, take her in your car."

Another pain ripped through Joanna and she gasped, reaching for Michael's hand, grateful he was here. "Hang on, hon," he said, giving her hand a reassuring squeeze. "I'll get you to the hospital in five minutes." He turned to Danny. "Go get my car, pull it around front."

"What can I do?" Patrick asked, gaping at Joanna with a combination of curiosity and concern.

"You call Dr. Summers," Maeve instructed.

"I'll go one better," Patrick said. "I'll go get him. Michael, I'll meet you at the hospital," he said as he sprinted toward the door.

"Maeve," Joanna said softly, biting her lip as tears filled her eyes. "I'm sorry I ruined the shower."

Maeve and Michael exchanged glances. Only Joanna would be concerned about something so trivial, when she might possibly be in labor.

"Hon," Michael said, going down on his haunches. "I'm going to pick you up and carry you to the car, is that all right?" He was almost afraid to touch her, afraid of causing her more pain.

Still biting her lip, Joanna nodded as he lifted her in his arms. "Wait, Michael. My suitcase."

"We'll get it later," he said, striding toward the door with her in his arms. He could feel her trembling as the contractions hit. Outside, Danny had the car running and the back door open. Michael climbed in the back with Joanna in his arms. "Let's hit it, Danny," he ordered, shutting the door firmly.

Enclosed in Michael's arms, Joanna stretched her legs out, hoping it would ease the pain.

Shaken, Michael held her as she closed her eyes, leaned her head against his shoulder and bit her lip. Feeling helpless, he leaned his forehead against hers. "Don't worry, hon, everything's going to be fine." It had to be. It just had to be.

"It's too soon, Michael," Joanna said, trying not to cry. She promised herself she'd be calm, but she was failing miserably. She was terrified, not just for herself, but for her baby as well. "It's too soon for the baby. Something's wrong."

"Don't worry," he said again, brushing his lips across her forehead. "You and the baby are going to be just fine. I promise." It was a promise he prayed he could keep.

By the time Maeve and Da made it to the hospital, Michael, Danny and Patrick were pacing the waiting room.

"How is she?" Maeve asked, going to Michael. She could see the worry, the fear in her son's eyes and it broke her heart.

Dragging a shaky hand through his hair, he shook his head. "I don't know, Ma. Dr. Summers is still in there with her." He dropped his shaking hands into his pockets, hoping to steady them. "They won't let me see her." Maeve patted her son's arm.

"Don't worry, Dr. Summers is a good man and a better doctor. She's in good hands, Michael. You'll only be in the way, son."

Frustrated, he blew out a breath, looking over his mother's head toward the door. "Yeah, but why hasn't he told us anything? He's been in there for almost half an hour."

Maeve shrugged, trying to keep her tone light. "When there's something to tell us, he will. Babies come in their own time, Michael." She smiled, trying to lighten his mood. "They don't come equipped with watches, so they move at their own pace, without a care as to whom they're inconveniencing."

"Wonderful," Michael said dryly, resuming his pacing as his mother found a seat. He felt like an animal that had been caged too long. A million thoughts ran through his mind; a million memories.

Joanna the day he'd told her about Brian.

The first day he'd taken her to the doctor's office.

Shopping for maternity clothes with her, laughing at her rather humorous descriptions of the clothing available.

The night of the St. Patrick's Day party. How beautiful she had looked; how sweet she had smelled. He'd give anything now to be able to see her, to hear her laugh, to smell her perfume.

Anything.

"Michael?"

He whirled. Dr. Summers stood in the doorway. Michael covered the room in three quick strides. "How is she?"

Dropping an arm around Michael's shoulder, Dr. Summers steered him to a quiet corner. "Michael, she's in active labor. She developed a leak in her water bag."

"Is that a problem?" Michael's worried eyes searched the doctor's.

"Yes," he said bluntly. "We don't know how long the bag's been leaking, that means the baby's natural immunity might be gone. If infection has set in, and we don't know that yet, it could be very damaging to the baby. We could be dealing with blindness, deafness. It's hard to tell."

"Oh God." Michael's insides twisted as he dragged a hand through his hair again. This couldn't be happening. It couldn't be. Dread rolled over him. He'd promised he'd take care of her and the baby.

He'd failed once again.

The knowledge seared him as bile rose in his throat. This couldn't be happening; it couldn't be.

Dr. Summers had warned them. He knew there was a possibility of complications. He should have taken it more seriously. He should have done more to protect her and the baby. If he had, perhaps this wouldn't have happened.

The thought made him feel physically sick.

He'd failed her.

"We have a decision to make." Dr. Summers slipped his hands into his coat pocket. "If we take the baby now with the complications Joanna's had, it might be too small to survive the birth process. Joanna's only in her seventh month and from what we can tell, the baby's not that big.

Maybe three and a half pounds. But if we try to stop labor and try to have her hold off delivery for a few weeks, until the baby is stronger, bigger, we'll run the risk of infection setting in and doing permanent damage to the child.''

Michael's grim gaze searched the doctor's. "So what you're saying is either way we lose.''

"It's not that dismal, Michael. I've had worse cases, but I won't sugarcoat it. Joanna's in a tough spot.''

Michael felt as if his heart had slowed in his chest. He had a feeling the doctor wasn't telling him something. "She's going to make it, isn't she? I mean, women have babies every day.'' He took a step closer, his fists balled. "Tell me Joanna's going to be all right!''

"I'm sorry, Michael.'' The doctor shook his head. "I can't guarantee it. Her blood pressure is sky-high right now. That's always a dangerous situation in a pregnant woman. We're doing our best to bring it down, but since she's in active labor, we have to be extremely careful of the measures we take so we don't do any damage to the baby. I'm sure the stress of her situation has contributed to the rise in her pressure.'' Dr. Summers paused, his face grim. "Michael, I'm sorry, but there is a possibility we could lose Joanna and the baby.''

"Oh God.'' Desperation clawed at him. Michael whirled away, unable and unwilling to comprehend what the doctor had just told him. He whirled back around, grabbing the lapels of the doctor's white coat and nearly lifting him off of his feet.

"She has to make it, Doc.'' His voice hard and firm, Michael gave the doctor a shake, nearly rattling the man's teeth. "She *has* to be all right, do you hear me?'' For the first time since his father had died, Michael found tears in his eyes. "You can't let Joanna die. You can't. Do you understand me? Not Joanna. Not the baby. Do you hear me?'' He shook the doctor again, his voice rising. "Tell me they're both going to be all right!''

"Easy, Mikey,'' Da said, dropping a large, heavy hand

on Michael's shoulder. "The doctor will do his best, son."
He moved closer to his grandson. "Let him go, Mikey,"
he said quietly, laying his arthritic hands over his grandson's and easing them from the doctor's coat. It took some
effort. "Let him go, son," he soothed, his voice as gentle
as a soft mist. "Let him go, lad, so he can see to Joanna."
His voice was comforting. He knew the ache the lad felt.
His own Molly had lost a child and he thought he'd go
mad with the pain. Even after all these long years, he still
ached with it. "He'll do his best, Mikey. He'll do his
best." Da took Michael's hands in his own, holding them
steady in comfort for a moment.

"I want to see her," Michael demanded. He felt small
and helpless for the first time in his life. "I *have* to see
her."

"Normally I'd say no," Dr. Summers said. "But she
wants to see you, Michael." Dr. Summers dropped a comforting hand to Michael's shoulder. "She's been doing
nothing but asking for you. I think you might be the only
person to calm her, and right now, Michael, it's imperative
that she stay calm so that she can make an intelligent decision as to what she wants us to do about the baby." The
doctor looked at Michael carefully. "It's her call, Michael.
It has to be. It's her child."

Nodding, Michael quietly followed Dr. Summers down
the hall toward a labor room. He took a long, deep breath,
then wiped a hand across his face, before pushing open
the door.

Eyes closed, she looked small and fragile laying in the
bed with monitors seemingly hooked up everywhere, beep-
ing ominously. Quietly he walked to the bed, knowing his
legs were barely holding him up. Fear unlike anything he'd
ever known had sapped his strength. He glanced down at
her and swallowed hard, feeling his aching heart constrict.

He was almost afraid to touch her, afraid to cause her
any more pain. Gently he touched her hand, bending down
close so she could hear him.

"Joanna?" Even though his voice was a whisper, it echoed loudly in the room.

"Michael." Opening her eyes, she reached for his hand, trying to smile. She simply couldn't manage it. "Oh, Michael."

"Shh, shh, don't cry, hon." He brushed the hair off her damp forehead, then wiped her tears. "Don't cry."

"Michael, did they tell you?" She sniffled, clinging even tighter to his hand. "About the baby?"

"Yeah, I just talked to Dr. Summers."

Her eyes searched his as she clung to his hand as if it were a lifeline, grateful he was there. "Michael, I don't know what to do. I'm so scared." She began to cry in earnest. "I'm going to lose the baby."

Michael slid his arms around her, gently holding her close, whispering softly to her. "You're not going to lose the baby, Joanna. Now come on, hon, don't cry."

"I'm scared, Michael," she whispered again, clinging to him tighter. Tears slipped unheeded down her face. "So scared. I don't know what I'd do if I lose this baby." The thought was inconceivable.

She clung to Michael, not caring that at the moment she needed him, needed his strength and his calm more than she'd ever needed anything or anyone in her life. In that instant she realized just how much she'd come to need and depend on Michael.

"Don't be scared, hon. I'm here. Everything is going to be fine." His own eyes grew damp again as he realized the seriousness of the situation. "You just have to try to calm down." He rested his brow against hers. "Dr. Summers is a good doctor, hon," he whispered, brushing his lips against her forehead and stroking away her tears. Her face was flushed and felt unbearably warm. "Everything will be fine." His words sounded hollow to his own ears.

"You'll get through this, Joanna, just like you've gotten through everything else the past seven months." He pressed another kiss to her temple, holding her, rocking her gently. "You're strong—stronger than you think. Don't give up now." He touched her stomach. "She's counting on you."

"I couldn't have gotten through any of this without you, Michael." Sniffling, she buried her face against his chest, clinging tightly to him, realizing just how true her statement was. He'd been through so much with her, everything almost from the beginning.

"Shh." He brushed a hand over her hair. His heart felt as if it was being ripped into tiny pieces. "Don't worry, hon." Helpless, he didn't know what to say.

"Michael." Dr. Summers strode into the room. "I need to check Joanna. I'm afraid you'll have to leave."

Quietly he nodded, not wanting to let go or leave. He feared he might never see her again. Maybe if he just held her, he could keep her and the baby safe.

"Michael." Dr. Summers laid a gentle hand on his back.

"All right." Swiping his own eyes, Michael drew back to look at Joanna. Their gazes met, held. She clung to him. Gently he pressed a soft kiss to her lips, holding her one last time. "I'll be waiting right outside." He squeezed her hand. "However long it takes, I'll wait. Do you understand?"

"Yes, Michael." She wiped her eyes, not wanting him to leave, but knowing he couldn't stay. The doctor had already explained that Michael couldn't be in the delivery room as they'd planned because of the complications she'd developed.

Michael stopped at the door and turned for one last look at her. His heart ached so much he had an actual physical pain in his chest.

Their gazes met, clung. Michael felt a fist squeeze his heart. She looked so small, so scared, he didn't want to leave her. She'd faced so much alone in her life, he couldn't bear for her to have to face this alone as well.

"I'll be here for you, Joanna. No matter what. No matter how long it takes, I'll be here."

Forcing his feet to move, Michael reluctantly turned and headed down the hall with nothing left for him to do but wait.

Time seemed to slow to a standstill. After five and a half hours, Michael's frustration level was at an all-time high. He hadn't seen Dr. Summers since he'd told him Joanna had made a decision; they were going to go ahead and deliver the baby.

As the sixth hour came and went, Michael found his strength and energy sapped and he sank into a chair next to his mother. She patted his arm.

"It's always hard to watch someone you care about in pain, son."

Blowing out an exasperated breath, he took the cup of coffee his brother Danny passed to him. "I know, Ma—" He broke off and looked at her over the rim of his paper coffee cup as he took a sip of the steaming brew. It tasted bitter on his tongue. "I feel so helpless."

"It's not your fault, Michael," she said softly, laying her hand on his arm. "Nothing could have prevented this."

Frustrated, he dragged a hand through his hair. "Ma, I *should* have known. I should have done more. Dr. Summers told us how dangerous it was." He blew out a frustrated breath, glancing at the clock again.

"You're not responsible, Michael." Maeve shook her head. "Nay, not for this."

Michael grunted, sipping his coffee. It had done little to ease the sick feeling in his gut. "I—"

"Michael." His mother's tone of voice stopped him cold. "I'll not have you taking responsibility or accepting guilt for something you couldn't control. A baby is a miracle, conceived by man, approved by the Almighty. Not even you could have stopped or prevented this, son."

"But, Ma, I made a promise—"

"Aye, it's your promises again, Michael." Sadly she nodded. "You had no right to promise something you had no control over, son. As I see it, you made a promise and you kept it. You agreed to look after Joanna and her un-born child. You did your job. No one could have done better, but this…" She waved her hand in the air. "'Tis not your fault, son. Not your fault at all. Babies have a way of coming on their own timetable, not ours. This one's apparently ready to be born."

"I let her down, Ma," he said softly, rubbing his hands over his tired eyes. They were burning.

"Nay, son, I don't agree and I don't think Joanna would, either. You were a fine and good friend to her, Michael. You should be proud."

Proud.

The word reverberated in his mind. Proud wasn't what he was feeling at the moment. If anything happened to Joanna or the baby… He let the thought trail off, unable to finish it.

"Michael?" Dr. Summers stood in the doorway of the waiting room. Michael was on his feet in an instant, crossing the room in three long strides. Dr. Summers had known him for years, but still he backed up a step.

"Well?"

Dr. Summers smiled. "She's weak, lost a lot of blood, but all in all she's fine."

Michael nearly sagged to the ground in relief. "And the baby?"

Dr. Summers smile broadened. "She fooled us all. The baby's small, four pounds eleven ounces, but it looks like she's going to be just fine. She has a few problems from her prematurity, but nothing she can't overcome with time. We've taken her up to Neonatal Intensive Care just as a precautionary measure. She'll have to stay in the hospital a few weeks, but I don't anticipate any problems. She should be just fine with a little weight and a little time."

"She?" Feeling giddy, Michael blew out a breath, running a hand through his hair. He felt as if someone had drained all his blood, then pumped it back in again. *"She?"*

The doctor nodded. "It's a girl, Michael. A beautiful, red-haired bouncing baby girl." Dr. Summers grinned, then let out a squeal when Michael grabbed him in a bear hug and twirled him around the room.

"Thanks, Doc." He set the man down on his feet. "Thanks."

"Can I see Joanna?" Michael asked.

"Just for a minute. She's exhausted. But I think seeing you might do some good." He watched Michael sprint from the room. "Just for a minute," he called. "Stop at the nurses' station and they'll tell you the room number."

"So it's a girl," Maeve said, coming to kiss the doctor on the cheek and take his hands in hers. "Your father would have been proud of you." She kissed him again.

Maeve laughed, watching Da, Danny and Patrick who were busy slapping each other on the back, as if they'd had a hand in the successful birth and delivery.

"A girl you say," Da said, pumping the doctor's hand. "Aye, a redheaded girl child, and me caught without my cigars." He beamed proudly, turning to his grandsons. "A girl," he repeated. "Come on, lads, we've a fine, fine reason to celebrate."

"Joanna?"

Pushing open the door, Michael's eyes lasered in on her. She was laying in the middle of the bed. Her eyes were closed, her hair damp. She looked pale and drained, and terribly small, but he was absolutely certain he'd never seen anything or anyone more beautiful.

"Joanna, it's me," he whispered, going to her and laying his hand over her limp one. He felt a little frightened and in awe, knowing what she'd just been through.

Her eyes fluttered open and she smiled a beautiful smile. There was a radiant glow about her, almost an ethereal beauty radiating from her. She looked so happy, so peaceful.

And so incredibly exhausted.

"Michael." His name whispered out as her eyes filled with joyous tears. Hormones shifting, emotions rising, she lifted her arms to him, needing to hold him and be held by him.

Grinning, and feeling an explicable euphoria, Michael instinctively gathered her in his arms, and held her close, savoring her scent, her closeness. He could hear the slow, steady beat of her heart against his. It was the most reassuring thing he'd ever felt in his life. He thought he was going to lose her. And until this moment he hadn't realized how very necessary she'd become to his life.

A hint of panic rose at the thought, but he pushed it back, pressing a kiss to the top of her head, then trailing a line of grateful kisses down her temple, her cheek.

Tilting her head back, she glanced up at him. "It's a girl, Michael. A beautiful little girl."

"I know, hon. I know." He held her tight, letting go of the fear he'd held in check. "God, I was so scared." He'd never admitted the words aloud before. He'd never had the courage to admit it to anyone. With Joanna he did. "So incredibly, utterly scared." Instinctively, he tightened his arms around her as if he could keep her safe.

All of these months, all that they'd been through, it had never occurred to him that he could lose her. When faced with the prospect, it had simply paralyzed him. Joanna had become so much a part of his life that he couldn't even imagine life without her.

He'd been too busy burying his emotions to face them. But now, they bubbled unbidden to the surface and he could no longer ignore them. But now wasn't the time for talk. That would come later, after they'd both had some sleep and some time.

"I'm so proud of you." His chest was bursting with pride and he didn't know why. He drew back to look at her, still grinning like a fool. "You did it, Joanna. You did it."

She tried to lift her head, but she simply couldn't manage it. She did manage a ghost of a smile as she snuggled closer to him, feeling incredibly, unbelievably happy...and safe.

"No, Michael, we did it." Her gaze sought his and she knew she could no longer control the emotions that had been threatening all these months, emotions she'd tried so hard to keep on a tight rein. "I couldn't have done it without you." Tears swam in her eyes again. "I don't know how to thank you, to tell you—" Her voice broke as emotions swarmed, then overwhelmed her. How could she ever put into words what he'd meant to her? How much she appreciated everything he'd done for her?

"You and your family..." She paused to sniffle, wiping her nose with the tissue he offered, then gave up and gave in to the tears, nearly overpowered by the feeling racing through her. She clung to him, clutching his shirt in her fingers, wanting to hold on to him forever.

She knew better than to want, to yearn, but someone forgot to tell her aching, battered heart. Wrapped in his arms, she knew she'd never wanted anything as much as she wanted him. Not just as a friend, not just for a few months, but...forever.

"Shh, honey, don't cry." Normally a woman's tears made him uneasy. But these were tears of joy, of happiness, and this was Joanna. Her tears moved him. "You don't have to thank me." He brushed her hair off her face, kissing the top of her head again. He realized it wasn't gratitude he wanted from her, but something far more. Something he wasn't certain he had a right to want or expect.

Joanna sniffled, taking the tissue he'd pulled from the box on the nightstand and, blowing her nose again, trying to gather and control her emotions.

"I think I'm going to call her Emma. What do you think, Michael?"

Laughing, he dragged a hand of relief through his hair. "Honey, after what we've been through, I don't care if you call her Bad-Tempered Brunhilda." He grinned at her amused expression, touching her cheek. "But Emma's a beautiful name."

For the first time all day Joanna laughed. She was so inexplicably exhilarated and exhausted and happy. So very, very happy. She finally had what she'd longed for her whole life: a family.

But something was missing.

Nervous, she chewed her lower lip. "Michael, I don't know what's going to happen now, but I just want you to know that I could never have done this...gone through all of this the past few months without you."

She was fine and so was the baby, and she had no idea if she'd even see Michael again. The mere thought brought a sharp pain to her heart.

"Thank you, Michael, for everything." She licked her lips, which were dry and almost cracked from the long labor and delivery. She hadn't been allowed even a glass of water, only shaved ice, which did little to appease her thirst. "I—we." She corrected herself. "I don't even know how to put into words what everything you've done for us means. Oh, Michael."

He didn't say anything. He just gathered her close, letting her rest her head on his chest, holding her tightly against him again. At least this part he was prepared for; he'd read about the weepiness after birth in one of the books he'd gotten from the library.

"Don't cry, hon." He brushed the hair off her face, and gently laid her down on the bed. "You've had quite a day. Dr. Summers wants you to get some rest."

"Are you going home?" Smiling, and a bit embarrassed at her show of emotions, she sniffled again, dragging the covers up.

"I was." He looked so uncertain she wanted to grin. "Unless you need something? Do you want me to stay?"

"No." She smiled. "I'm fine. But could you bring my suitcase back in the morning? I'll need some of my stuff. The baby's going to have to stay in the hospital for a few weeks, but Dr. Summers said I can go home in a day or so depending on how things go."

He took her hand and he kissed it. "I'll be happy to bring your suitcase in the morning. Anything else you need?"

You, Michael. I need you. The words whispered through her mind, stunning her, but she was far too weary to fight them.

"No, thanks. I think I just need some…sleep." Her energy was waning and fatigue was slowly stealing over her, zapping what was left of her strength.

He kissed her forehead. "Go to sleep, hon. I'll be back in the morning. With your suitcase." Tucking her hand under the blanket, he waited a moment, until he was certain she was asleep, then quietly tiptoed out of the room, wondering why the thought of going home alone to an apartment without Joanna suddenly made him feel so inexplicably…empty.

Chapter Ten

Michael groaned at the bright sunlight as he stepped out of his car in the hospital parking lot, wishing the pack of elephants dancing in his head would take a rest. He'd joined Da and his brothers in celebrating last night, and apparently he'd celebrated a bit too much, if the pounding in his head and the dryness of his mouth was any indication.

It was almost noon. He'd overslept, simply because he hadn't crawled into bed until nearly dawn. Or at least he hadn't crawled onto the floor. He hadn't quite made it to the bed.

News of the birth of little Emma had spread like wildfire through the neighborhood and the station, courtesy of Mrs. O'Bannion who felt it her duty to tell everyone she had ever known. As a result, when he went to get a pass to Joanna's room, he had to wait since she already had visitors.

Sauntering into the coffee shop, Michael picked up the morning paper, and a steaming cup of coffee, hoping it would steady his hands and his nerves. With coffee in hand, he wandered into the gift shop as he waited. A large purple stuffed teddy bear caught his eye and he found himself grinning. The bear would probably be bigger than Emma for at least a decade, but it was so adorable he couldn't resist.

With his coffee, newspaper and his new purple friend in tow, Michael went to the lobby to wait.

When Tomas and his partner walked off the elevator Michael felt a flutter of panic. It always made him nervous when Joanna was with someone from the station, especially someone from his unit because he worried they'd say too much about the day Brian died.

"Lieutenant." Tomas shook his hand, grinning at the large teddy bear cradled in his arms. "Joanna looks wonderful. Radiant. We couldn't see the baby yet, but Joanna has a picture and Emma is a beauty just like her mother." Tomas heartily patted his back. "It is good now that this is over. You're a wonderful man and have done a very honorable thing. I'm sure Joanna is very grateful to have you as a friend, to know that you have honored and fulfilled your promise to her late husband." Another elevator opened and a crowd pushed out, separating him and Tomas, preventing Michael from questioning him about what he'd said to Joanna.

A wave of panic tightened Michael's throat. Tossing his coffee into the nearest trash can, he ignored the elevator and took the stairs two at a time, his nerves screaming.

When he walked into Joanna's room, he was surprised to find her sitting up. When she glanced up he saw that her eyes were red-rimmed and puffy. They were also filled with pain. An alarm bell went off in his head.

"Joanna?" He stepped into the room, feeling a cold sense of dread the moment he saw her. "What's wrong?"

Joanna's heart leapt at the sight of him, then settled like a stone in her chest. She couldn't bear to look at him. She simply couldn't. If she did, she knew she'd come apart.

Instead she busied herself with the satin trim on her

blanket, pleating and unpleating it, trying very hard to control her feelings. Anguish filled her heart, her soul. Seeing Michael only made it worse.

"Joanna?" His gaze searched hers. "What is it?" He was standing over her, feeling ridiculous because he was cradling a large purple teddy bear. He set it on the bed.

"You lied to me, Michael." Her voice was soft and full of sorrow as she finally raised her gaze to his. The look in her eyes, the raw pain nearly took his breath away. He felt as if he'd taken a bullet to the gut.

He took a slow, deep breath, trying to remain calm. He didn't even bother to pretend he didn't know what she was talking about. He wouldn't insult her that way.

"Joanna, listen to me." He tried to take her hand.

She shrunk back from him. She couldn't bear if he touched her, not now, not when she knew the truth. "No, Michael. You listen to me." Her throat was clogged with grief, with tears. "Tomas told me you made a promise to Brian, a promise to look after me and the baby." Her eyes searched his, pleading with him to say it was a lie, a misunderstanding, anything but the truth. "Is it true?"

The question hung in the air for a long, silent moment.

"Yes," he said quietly, his voice strained and low. His fists clenched in frustration. He'd hurt her; he could see it in her face, her eyes. His own heart ached with the knowledge. He'd never meant to hurt her. He'd only wanted to protect her.

The knowledge wasn't much comfort now.

"But it's not what you think."

Her throat tightened at his words, but she swore she wouldn't cry. Not in front of him. She wouldn't let him know how this had hurt her, cut her to the quick. And she certainly didn't want any more of his charity.

"Why didn't you tell me?" Her gaze searched his. "Why, Michael?"

"I didn't want to hurt you." He dragged a hand through

his hair. "What was done was done. It wouldn't bring Brian back."

"No," she said quietly, "it wouldn't. But you lied to me, Michael. After you asked me to trust you."

Her accusation made him flinch and he took a step closer. She held up her hand to stop him, and he noted her hand was shaking.

"No, don't." Her voice was an empty whisper. Her eyes huge in her pale face "Don't come any closer, please." She looked up at him, clutching the satin trim of the blanket tight in her fingers. "You asked me to trust you, Michael, and I did," she said quietly, unable to stop the tears that had been threatening. Her voice was devoid of emotion, as if it was echoing down a long, empty tomb. He remembered the last time her voice sounded like that, and hated the fact that he had done that to her.

"You deliberately lied to me, and betrayed that trust even after you promised me you never would." She lifted stricken eyes to his, unable to understand how he could have done such a thing to her. "How could you do that to me, Michael?" Tears slipped unheeded down her face. "How?"

Desperate, he dragged a hand through his hair. Each word was like a sword in his heart. "No. It wasn't like that. It wasn't deliberate. You have to believe me."

She looked at him for a long, silent moment. "*Have* to believe you?" The words hung heavy in the air for a moment. She wanted to shout at him, to rage but she couldn't. She was too stunned, too hurt, in too much pain. Nothing had ever hurt like this. Nothing. She took a deep, shaky breath. "I believed you once, Michael. Because you asked me to. I also trusted you because you asked me to. It's a mistake I won't ever repeat again." She swallowed around the lump in her throat and dared a glance at him. There was something she had to know. "Did your family know about your promise, Michael? Did your family know that you had agreed to look after another man's burden?"

"Joanna, you're not, you were never—"

"Did your family know?" she demanded, and he sighed heavily. "Did they?" Hurt and betrayal echoed in every word.

"They knew," he admitted softly, wishing he could turn back the clock and change things.

"Oh my God." Her hand went to her mouth and her head fell back. She couldn't stop the silent tears that tracked down her face. Humiliation warred with shame.

"Joanna, that's not how it was." He had to make her understand. "Please give me a chance to explain."

"What's to explain?" She lifted her head to stare at him. Her heart felt as if someone had shattered it into a million pieces.

"All these months, Michael, while I've been living with you, everyone knew the truth but me. You made me think you were my friend, that you cared about me and the baby. Now I find out you only did it because of some deathbed promise you made. I was nothing more than a burden to you. Just another one of Michael's responsibilities. But this time you even dragged your whole family into the act." Mortified and humiliated, she couldn't stop the tears from flowing. "How could you do that to me, Michael? How? Especially knowing how I felt about being a burden to someone, let alone to your whole family."

"No!" The word tore out of him and he reached for her hand. She wouldn't let him touch her.

"Please, Michael." She laid her head back down and closed her eyes, wanting to be alone with her pain. "Please just leave me alone."

"No, not until you hear me out." He dragged a shaky hand through his hair, hating the fact that he'd dredged up old memories for her as well as old pain. And then added to it. He felt like a heel.

"You were never an obligation or responsibility." His voice was firm with passion. He had to make her believe him. "Never."

She lifted her head. Her red-rimmed eyes searched his. "Then why didn't you just tell me the truth from the beginning, Michael? Why?"

"I never meant to lie to you. Believe me, I thought I was doing what was best." Tension tore through him and Michael rolled his shoulders, trying to ease it.

"Best for who?" she accused.

"For you, of course." He felt numb. Totally numb. "I would never do anything to hurt you. Not ever." His eyes pleaded with her to believe him.

"But you did, Michael," she said softly, her eyes swimming with tears.

She'd spent the past few moments in shock, shock that the man she thought she knew, the man she thought she could trust could have lied to her, deceived her all these months. She felt like a fool. A complete, total fool. She took a deep breath, still keeping her hands busy with the blanket.

"You lied to me, and you deceived me. It's... unforgivable." Her voice broke and she shook her head, holding a hand up as he reached for her. "I thought you were an honorable man. Obviously I was mistaken."

Her words cut him to the core. Nothing she could have said could have wounded him more. He'd spent his whole life trying to be honorable, responsible, trying to do the right thing.

And he'd failed miserably once again.

"I think you should at least let me explain." His mouth was a hard, tight line. "There's more to it than what's on the surface. You at least owe me that."

She glanced at him sharply, sorely tempted to tell him she owed him nothing, but she banked her temper, deciding he was right. She'd hear him out.

"Fine, Michael. Explain."

He took a deep breath. "I never told you what happened the day Brian died. Well, I think it's time you knew." He paused, considering his words. He decided he wasn't going to sugarcoat it. Any of it. She had a right to hear the truth, and he had to be the one to tell her.

"Internal Affairs Division and the Feds had been investigating my unit for months. I had come up clean, perfectly clean, but they knew someone in my unit had been taking payoffs from some of the bigger drug dealers in exchange for information about busts, evidence, that kind of thing." He took a deep breath, then went on. "They would have no way of knowing the kind of information they did unless someone in the unit was tipping them off in exchange for cash."

Nausea swept through her and she felt a wave of horror. "Brian?"

Michael nodded. "I swear to you I didn't know it at the time. Maybe if I did I would have handled it differently. If there was a bad cop in my unit I wanted him out. The men in my unit have to depend on one another, trust each other, sometimes with their lives. We can't afford to have a bad cop. It could cost someone their life." Inhaling slowly, he tried to calm the feelings of anger and frustration that were still with him.

"We had a huge bust scheduled. We'd been working on the case for over seven months. Two of my men had gone undercover, we'd gotten them out just a few days before the raid or there would have been more cops dead. We knew that a huge shipment of heroin was coming in from China. It took us four days to set everything up. It was four days of long nights, cold coffee and no sleep." He sighed. "Brian hadn't been in for those four days. He'd sat in on the preliminary meetings about the raid, but that was the last we saw of him. He was on the duty roster but no one knew where he was. I was so busy and so bogged down I didn't give it much thought. Sometimes I'll go days without seeing one of my men, especially if we're working on different cases and different shifts." He glanced at her. "I'd hoped I'd never have to tell you this, Joanna."

"Just tell me the truth, Michael." Her eyes pleaded with him. "Please?"

Michael inhaled slowly, knowing how much this was going to hurt her, but unable to prevent it. "Brian, umm, got involved with...with—"

"Another woman, Michael?"

He nodded. She didn't look shocked or surprised as he'd expected. Maybe she knew more than he'd given her credit for. "Yeah." He blew out a frustrated breath. "She wasn't from the neighborhood. No one you would know." It was important that she know at least that much. "She had a nasty heroin habit, a very expensive one. We figured somewhere around a couple of hundred a day."

Her hand flew to her mouth in shock, in horror. "Oh my God."

"I guess Brian went on the take to support her habit." He shrugged. "She had an apartment somewhere over near Palmer Court." He mentioned a neighborhood bordering Logan Square. "I guess that's where Brian had been staying when he didn't come home."

The nausea rolled in her stomach. Her husband had a whole separate life she knew nothing about. The betrayal burned deep. She knew there had been other women, but she hadn't known he had a whole other life that didn't include her.

"Anyway, the day of the raid, like I said Brian was on the duty roster, but no one knew where he was. He was supposed to be with us, but when we put the wheels in motion he was nowhere to be found." He shook his head. "They knew we were coming, Joanna. Someone had tipped them off, but apparently not soon enough for them to get rid of everything. They still had enough illegal guns and drugs to put all of them away for a very long time." Sighing, he shook his head, trying to dislodge the painful memories.

"What happened, Michael?"

"They were waiting for us. Three of my men were hit

before we even broke down the door.'' He rubbed a hand over his face, startled that the memories were still so vivid and so painful. ''We'd called for backup, but until then we were on our own. Shots were flying everywhere. We had them cornered in one room, but out of the corner of my eye, I saw a lone figure run across the hallway. I fired.'' He raised his gaze to hers.

''It was Brian.'' His voice was achingly soft. ''I killed him.'' His words reverberated like a cannon in the quiet room. ''I'm the one who killed your husband, Joanna.''

Michael was miserable.

For three long, lonely nights and days he paced the length of his apartment until he'd nearly worn out the linoleum. It had been three days since his confession to Joanna. After he'd told her the truth, she merely asked him to leave. She hadn't screamed, yelled or cried; it was as if everything inside of her had died.

Nothing had ever hurt so much.

He'd tried to talk to her, to explain, but she'd turned her head, closed her eyes, and merely asked him to leave.

He had no choice. Desolate, he'd left, knowing that like everyone else in her life, he, too, had betrayed her. The knowledge nearly made him ill.

Pacing the length of his apartment, he thought about getting drunk, if only to ease the pain in his gut, then realized he didn't have the energy. Besides, it wouldn't help matters.

All these months he thought Joanna needed him, never realizing that he needed her just as much.

He couldn't face the fact that she might not be a part of his life anymore.

He loved her, he realized belatedly. Loved Joanna. And little Emma.

All these months he'd been a blind fool.

He'd spent all this time burying his feelings, his emotions, but now, they all came bubbling to the surface and he realized with stark bitterness what he'd been afraid to face all along: He loved Joanna. Not like a friend. Not out of some ridiculous sense of responsibility. But like a woman. A woman who was meant for him.

How the hell could he have not seen it?

Maybe because he was so busy trying to be responsible, so busy trying to bury all his emotions so that he could do what he thought was right, he couldn't see anything but his own fear.

What a fool!

Joanna was as much a part of him as his blood, his breath. He'd been so wrapped up in making sure he didn't let her down, he'd blindly ignored what had been right in front of his face, his eyes, in his heart.

He'd never felt so lonely, so empty. The world seemed to have lost its luster.

How could he not have known he was hopelessly in love with her?

He was afraid to face his own feelings. Just as he'd been afraid to face them when his father died.

He couldn't bury them anymore.

He simply couldn't.

Now, he had no idea what he was going to do.

A knock at the door had him growling. He didn't want to see anyone. Didn't want to talk to anyone. In the past three days, Danny, Patrick and even Katie and his mother had all been up, trying to see to him, to talk to him, to comfort him. He didn't want comfort, or sympathy.

He wanted Joanna.

The door burst open. "Mikey, boy, what's it you're doing up here that's worrying your mother so?" Unmindful of the glare his grandson sent him, Da stepped into the apartment, shutting the door softly behind him.

"I'm fine, Da."

"Aye, I can see that lad." Cocking his head, Da inspected him with wise eyes. "Three days worth of beard. No food in your belly or a shower for longer than that.

You growling at the door like some wounded cub. Fine you are, son.'' Da nodded sagely. ''Aye, I can see it with my own eyes I can.''

''Da—''

''Mikey, let me tell you a story.'' Da paused, choosing his words carefully. ''Sometimes it's a wee bit of a burden to be a man. We think we have to be all these things for the lasses in our life.'' Da stroked his jaw. ''We think we have to be strong. We think we have to protect them. We think we have to take care of them.'' Da laughed. ''Sometimes we bring about our own misery, son. Aye, your late grandmother taught me something very important right before she left this world.''

At the mention of his grandmother, Michael stopped pacing and looked at his grandfather curiously, hearing the pain in his voice.

''What, Da?''

''Your lovely grandmother, she held my hand during those last few hours of her life, and she thanked me, son. Not for being strong, or for protecting her, or for taking care of her. She smiled, and said a woman could do those things for herself if she'd a mind to.'' Da paused. ''Mikey, my lovely gal, with her last breath, thanked me for loving her.'' There was still awe in his voice at the knowledge he was eternally grateful for.

Puzzled, Michael stared at his grandfather. ''That's... it?''

Da smiled. ''Aye, you see, son, we men, sometimes we put too little importance on the things that matter the most to women. It's not what we do *for* them, son, but how we *feel* about them.'' Da tapped his chest. ''It's what's here, in our hearts that truly matters.'' He shrugged. ''Blockheads we are sometimes, Mikey, and we don't realize it. We dismiss our feelings, thinking all that other nonsense is but a man's job, but aye, to a lass, Mikey, how we feel about them is the most important thing.'' He paused. ''To a woman, knowing and feeling loved by her man, aye, that's what makes her heart sing. And if you're lucky, son, it's a long, beautiful song." Da sighed in remembrance, sighing wistfully. "Aye, a long, beautiful song." Clearing his throat, Da dug into his pocket for his handkerchief and noisily blew his nose. Slipping his hanky back in his pocket, he glanced at his watch.

"Your ma's mentioned that Joanna's coming home today, son. If you hurry, you just might be able to catch her."

Michael needed no further prodding. He knew what he had to do. He turned and headed toward the door, only to have Da lay a gentle hand on his arm, stopping him.

"Son." Grinning, eyes twinkling, Da wrinkled his nose. "Three days it's been, lad, and I think a wee bit of a shower might be in order first."

Joanna slipped out of the elevator and headed back to her room to finish packing. She'd gone up to the Neonatal Intensive Care Ward to say goodbye to Emma. She was growing and getting healthier every day, and the doctors felt she could come home soon.

Although Joanna hated the thought of leaving her daughter, she was anxious to get home, anxious to start her new life, a life she knew she would face without Michael.

It hurt. More than anything she'd ever experienced.

He should have been here, she thought, fighting back tears. He'd been through so much with her. The past three days she'd done little more than cry, unable to believe that Michael had betrayed her.

More importantly, the past three days, she'd finally realized just how much a part of her life Michael had become. Until now, she hadn't realized how much she needed him, or depended on him.

Or how much she loved him.

The knowledge had sent her reeling.

All these months, she'd tried so hard to keep her feelings

and emotions under control. She'd tried so hard to deny what she'd been feeling simply because she'd been afraid—afraid to trust, afraid to love again, afraid to hope.

But the past three days without Michael, she'd suddenly felt more alone and empty than she ever had in her life. Perhaps because now she finally realized exactly what she'd been missing.

She'd gone over and over everything that had happened. Her shock over Michael's behavior, and his confession about Brian had eased, replaced by a certain understanding of why Michael had done what he'd done.

Knowing Michael, she understood how, on some level, he had been trying to protect her. That in his mind, he'd been doing the right thing. Perhaps his intentions were honorable, but his methods were wrong. She couldn't believe Michael would ever deliberately do anything to hurt her.

Things would have been so much simpler had he just told her the truth from the beginning. Now, so many things made sense. Why Brian's life insurance had been held up. Why everyone at the precinct seemed to avoid her. Why Michael never talked about the day Brian had died.

She pushed open the door to her room and came to a halt, her heart tripping over itself. Hope flared then died quickly at the sight of Michael.

"Hello." He was standing at the window. He turned to her, his eyes drinking her in. "How's the baby?"

She let the door close softly behind her. Nervous, she laced her hands together, praying she wouldn't start crying again. He looked wonderful, absolutely wonderful and her heart nearly broke with love for him.

"She's fine, Michael." She swallowed. "What are you doing here?" she asked softly.

"Just taking care of some unfinished business." He slipped his hands into his pockets so she wouldn't see how nervous he was.

"I see." She glanced around the room. "I'm just getting

ready to go home." Her eyes widened and anger raced through her. There was a pile of clothes tumbled on the bed. It took her a moment to realize what he'd done.

"Michael, why on earth did you dump all my clothes out?" Furious and confused, she walked toward the bed and began refolding clothes. She'd already finished packing up the entire room, and now she had to do it all over again. She glanced around the room. "And where did you put my suitcase? How on earth do you expect me to get my clothes home? Stuff them into a paper bag?" She glared at him. "If this is a joke, I'm really not amused."

"Nope. Not a joke," he said, rocking back on his heels and crossing his arms over his chest.

She stopped to glare at him. "Then would you mind telling me exactly what you're doing? I'm not really in the mood for this."

"What are you in the mood for, Joanna?" He grinned that mischievous grin, the one that made her heart take flight. "I thought once we got home we could order Chinese. Or maybe a pizza. How does that sound?"

Home. When we got home.

His words echoed over and over in her mind, but she refused to give them pause. He was up to something again, something he no doubt didn't plan on telling her. She'd had more than her fair share of Michael's little surprises.

"Ridiculous," she countered, still folding clothes and trying to ignore him. "It sounds completely ridiculous. I've had the baby, Michael. Your...responsibility is over. You've done your duty. It's not necessary for you to do anything further. As I told you before, I appreciate everything you've done for me. But it's over. I'm going home, Michael, to *my* home."

"Fine," he said with a shrug. "If you want to go to your home, we'll go to your home. Doesn't make any difference to me whose home we go to." He shrugged again. "I'm not fussy."

Clutching a handful of nightclothes, she whirled on him.

"Not we," she said carefully, her teeth clenched. She was holding on to her tenuous control. But just barely. "There is no *we*. It's just...me." She swallowed. "Me and Emma." She wasn't going to cry. She wasn't.

"Nope." He shook his head. "Afraid not." He took a step closer, taking the nightclothes out of her hand. "See, I've got this problem." Absently he scratched his stubbled chin. He'd showered, but hadn't bothered to take the time to shave. "I was a little dense here for a while and didn't realize that I was looking for a home as well."

She blinked in confusion. "Are you crazy?" she asked suspiciously.

"Not anymore." He laughed, shaking his head.

"Then what are you talking about, Michael? You have a home and a family. A huge, wonderful family." Pain laced her words.

"Nope. What I have is an apartment. A cold, empty lonely apartment. What I need is a *home*," he stated, ignoring her confusion. "The one place I belong with the one person I belong with." He reached out and touched her cheek, remembering Da's advice. "I love you, Joanna. Wherever you are is home. We belong together. You, me and little Emma." His heart was in his throat as he waited.

Tears swam in her eyes. "Michael." She didn't know what to say, didn't want to believe, afraid of being disappointed and hurt again.

He wiped away a tear from her cheek. "I know you might not believe me, but it's true." He laughed softly. "I can be a little thick sometimes, but Da says it's in the genes." He shrugged. "I'm a male, what can I say." His eyes searched hers, full of love, full of hope. "I didn't realize until it was almost too late how much I needed you, loved you." He took a deep breath.

She opened her mouth as tears fell. "No, don't say anything, Joanna." He pressed his lips gently to hers. "I know. I was wrong," he whispered, sadly shaking his head, hoping, praying she'd be able to forgive him. "I should have told you the truth, but I was afraid, hon. Afraid if you knew the truth about what happened the day Brian died you'd blame me. Hate me. I was afraid to lose you. And until a few days ago I didn't realize just how much.''

''Oh, Michael, I could never hate you.'' She lifted a hand to his cheek, her bruised, empty heart finally over-flowing with love. ''I understand why you did what you did. You were trying to protect me. I understand that now.''

''Do you remember the night I told you that one of the things I learned after my father died was that when you love someone anything you do for them isn't a burden or a responsibility, but merely an extension of that love?'' She nodded. ''You were never a burden or a responsibility, Joanna, because I've loved you all along. If I would have faced my feelings, my emotions, instead of burying them I would have known it a lot sooner, and saved us both a lot of grief.'' His hands tightened on her waist. ''You're a gift, a precious gift in my life.''

She choked back a sob, remembering the night she'd wondered what it would feel like to have someone feel that way about her. To think her presence was a gift, not a burden.

She looked at Michael, afraid to hope, afraid to trust. And then she knew with absolute certainty.

He loved her.

She could see it clearly in his eyes, on his face. How had she missed it all these months?

Perhaps because she'd been too afraid to hope, too afraid of disappointment. Standing here, looking at him with the knowledge fresh on his face, she was no longer afraid. The burden she'd carried for so long seemed to lift, and she suddenly felt free and happy. Happier than she'd ever felt in her life.

''Are you ever going to be able to forgive me? To trust

me?'' Fear tightened his throat. "Do you think you could ever love me?''

Emotions swamped her, filling her eyes, her heart. "Oh, Michael.'' She threw her arms around him, holding him tight. "I think I've always loved you.'' Ignoring the tears that slid down her cheeks, she pressed quick kisses to his face. "I love you, Michael. I was just afraid to admit it even to myself. Afraid to hope—''

He held her face in his hands, his eyes lovingly going over her. "I don't ever want you to be afraid of anything ever again. Not ever. We're a family. Me, you and Emma. We belong *together*. For me, home is wherever you are. I realize that now.'' He lifted her hand and kissed it. "I love you, Joanna.'' Drawing her closer until she was pressed tightly against him, he kissed her with all the passion and love he'd held in check for so long.

She'd forgiven him, he realized, his heart filling with hope, with love. It humbled him, and only made him love her more.

Still holding her, he reluctantly dragged his lips from hers. "Let's go see our daughter, and then go home, hon.'' He took her hand and started toward the door.

Feeling giddy and happier than she'd ever felt in her life, she wanted to laugh, to sing. Instead she dug in her heels.

"Wait, Michael.'' She pulled him to a stop. "My clothes.'' She glanced over her shoulder, still not understanding why he'd made such a mess. "I have to repack my clothes.''

"Ah, that's right.'' He released her hand. "Let me get your suitcase.'' He went to the small closet and opened the door, pulling out a large, wrapped present.

"What on earth is that, Michael?''

Still holding the package, he dared to take a step closer, knowing this was the most important thing he'd ever done. "Open it.'' He handed it to her.

"All right.'' Hesitantly she ran her hands over the beautiful wrapping paper. "It's so pretty," she said quietly. "It's almost a shame to ruin it."

"Ruin away," he encouraged, standing behind her and watching over her shoulder as she slowly unwrapped the present. She struggled with the top of the box, finally managing to free it. She looked at the gift, not quite certain what to make of it.

"Michael?" She shook her head. "I...I don't understand."

Michael reached around her and lifted out the gift. "It's a new suitcase." He set it down on the bed and turned her by the shoulders to face him, his gaze lovingly going over her face. "I threw the other one away. It was time, don't you think?"

She touched his face, loving him. Tears trembled on her lips. Her suitcase had symbolized empty dreams and false hope. It was gone. Over. Forever.

She ran her hands lovingly over the new suitcase. It was filled with love and dreams and a bright, happy future.

"Yes, Michael," she whispered, her heart so full with love she felt it would burst. "It was finally time."

He grabbed the new suitcase with one hand and her with the other. "Let's get you packed, hon. This is one suitcase you're never going to have to pack again. You're home, Joanna," he whispered. "We're both finally home."

Smiling, he watched as she grabbed up heaps of clothes and flung them haphazardly into the suitcase. When she was finished, she turned to him with a grin.

"I'm ready, Michael."

She'd been ready her whole life. Ready and waiting for him. Only him.

He kissed her cheek, reaching for her suitcase with one hand and her hand with the other. "Come on, let's go...home."

Home. They were going home.

She and little Emma would have a real home.

And Michael.

It had always been Michael.

He'd been what she'd been searching for, waiting for all these years. The other half of her.

Taking his hand, Joanna held on tightly. It didn't matter where they went. Home was wherever Michael and Emma were; she knew that now.

"I love you, Michael." She stood on tiptoe and kissed him until he groaned softly. "Let's go...home."

Epilogue

Their wedding was a true Sullivan family affair. With the pub filled to the rafters with various Sullivan cousins, nieces, nephews, aunts and uncles, Da gave Joanna away, insisting on carrying little Emma in his arms while he did. Maeve and Katie stood up for Joanna, while Danny and Patrick stood up for Michael. And so, on a fine Saturday morning in June, with the sun shining, and the entire family, neighborhood and precinct in attendance, Joanna and Michael recited their vows.

Dressed in an antique lace and silk gown Maeve had helped her shop for, Joanna stood with Michael in front of their family, their friends and their daughter, pledging their life, and their love.

The moment the ceremony was over, the rousing celebration began.

"It's a fine, fine day for a wedding celebration." Puffing on a large, smelly cigar, Da bent and kissed Joanna's cheek, his eyes shining in pride. "Now you're a tried-and-true Sullivan, one of the clan, as it should be."

Carefully he draped an arm around her shoulder, puffing

vigorously on his cigar, blowing a heavy stream of smoke in the air, hoping Maeve wouldn't spot him. He'd been ducking her all afternoon. A man should be able to enjoy a good cigar on the day of his first grandson's wedding.

He nodded. "You've made me a proud man, today, lass, a proud man, indeed." He glanced across the room where Emma was sleeping soundly in the Sullivan family cradle. "Aye, and a happy one as well." Grinning, he puffed out his chest in pride. "You've given me my first great-grandchild. And a redheaded girl at that." Beaming, he took another puff. "How lucky can a man be?"

"Da." Touched, Joanna stood on tiptoe and kissed his cheek. "I'm the lucky one. I love you," she said softly, her eyes misting. "Each and every one of you."

He drew back, truly perplexed. "But of course, lass. How could you not?" She started to laugh, hugging him tight.

"Sweetheart." Michael came up next to her, sliding his arm around her. He couldn't resist, he pressed a kiss to her lips. "Emma's up from her nap and fussing a bit." He was still a little nervous holding the baby because she was so small and his hands were so big. And clumsy. But he was getting the hang of it.

"I'll go." She started, but Da reached out a hand to stop her. "Aye, let me go, lass. It's time the wee one got to know her grandfather." Da started toward the baby, just as Michael reached out and plucked the cigar from his hand.

"She's too young to smoke, Da," Michael scolded, trying not to laugh. Pulling awkwardly on his cummerbund, Da mumbled something under his breath about ungrateful children as he made his way toward the cradle, which was sitting in a quiet corner of the pub.

At the sight of Emma, he grinned. "Aye, there you are, lassie." He lifted Emma in his arms, cradling her close.

"Now what's the trouble, love?" He nuzzled her close. "Aye, you're fussing because no one's attending to you, is that it?" He chuckled, finding an empty seat in a quiet spot of the bar. Holding Emma tight, Da looked around the room, his eyes drifting to his grandsons. Pride swelled his heart.

Mikey, so strong, so proud, and now with a family of his own.

And Danny, so stubborn and headstrong and, he thought with a laugh, so very much like him.

And then there was Patrick. The baby who was no longer a baby, but a grown man with a whole future in front of him.

He glanced down at Emma. And now there was a new generation of Sullivans to carry on their name, their traditions. Jock would have been proud of his boys. Yes, indeed.

"Lassie, it's time you learned about your clan. Ah, the Sullivan brothers, there were six of us and aye, we were a wild and handsome bunch, lassie." Laughing at his memories, Da glanced at the cradle, memories of his own youth flooding him. "A long, long time ago, well, lassie, one of the Sullivan brothers, and a handsome fellow at that, fell madly in love with a fine and beautiful lass." Eyes shining, Da glanced at the baby in his arms and at the cradle that had carried so many hopes, dreams and memories. "Well, this pretty little lass was named Molly and her hair was as red as yours and her smile just as sweet and charming." He sighed heavily, wishing for his cigar. "But alas, Molly, well, she was pledged and matched to another."

He grinned suddenly, remembering the mischief and mayhem that ensued. "But like I said, lassie, we were the Sullivan brothers and not known for accepting defeat. So one of the brothers, the one in love with Molly, cooked up a plan, and a fine, grand plan it was," Da said with a chuckle of remembrance. "He couldn't bear the thought of his love pledged to another, nor could he accept living his life without her. And so, on the night before her match, when all was quiet, he and his brothers snuck into her camp and stole her."

Shaking his head, Da laughed as the baby gurgled. "Aye, I knew you'd like this story. On that very night, his own brothers helped him spirit his love away from their homeland and onto a fishing boat that would begin a journey that would take them to their new homeland. America."

Da's eyes misted as he thought of that long ago day. "It was a journey of love and new beginnings. All they had to their names was this cradle, the one you've been resting in. See, the lad had always known he and Molly were destined for each other and he'd made the cradle as a wedding present, something to show his eternal love, something to pass on to future generations so they would always know of that love." His voice grew soft as he stroked the baby's fine, soft red hair. "They had a wonderful, happy life together, full of mischief and an abundance of love, until the day his Molly girl drew her last breath."

Sighing softly, Da kissed Emma's cheek, holding her close, feeling the ache in his heart. "And, lassie, I'll tell you a secret, it's not a day goes by that I don't miss her." Sniffling, Da smiled gently, stroking Emma's red hair, so like his Molly's as he glanced around at his family, the family he and Molly had created. "I'm sorry she's not here to see this day. To see the son of our son, and you, our first great-grandchild." Pulling out his handkerchief, Da swiped at his nose. "Aye, she would have loved you, lassie."

He reached out and stroked a hand over the cradle, a cradle he had carved so many years ago with so much love. "I love you, Molly," he whispered, stroking the cradle, and thinking about all the years and the tears and the memories. "Aye, Molly girl, after all these years, I still miss you." He glanced at Emma and smiled. "Aye, you would have been proud."

* * * * *

Turn the page for a preview of the next installment of LULLABIES AND LOVE, Danny Sullivan finally meets his match in BABY WITH A BADGE, coming May 1998 from Silhouette Romance.

Chapter One

Nothing scared Detective Danny Sullivan of Chicago Police Department's Gang Crime Unit. Rumored to have nerves of steel, nothing had ever disturbed Danny's sense of peace and calm.

Being dateless on a Friday night might *worry* him.

Cracking up his mint '67 Corvette would probably *annoy* him.

A beautiful six-foot blonde might *intrigue* him.

But scare him? Not a thing in this world.

Except perhaps for the squirming little bundle of joy he found abandoned in the front seat of his unmarked squad car.

In the twilight of this warm Friday evening, Danny stood in front of the driver's door of his car, scowling, not certain his eyes weren't deceiving him. Blinking, it took a moment for things to register.

Someone had left a baby in his car.

Scrambling for his keys, Danny quickly unlocked the driver's-side door and slid in, his heart racing in panic as he hurriedly unrolled the window to let some fresh air in.

Seated in some kind of kid contraption, the baby was facing toward the back seat, cooing and kicking its feet, sucking on a soft, plastic toy ring, apparently pleased as punch about something.

Hesitantly, Danny touched him or her to see if there was a note, some identification—anything that would give him a clue as to who the child was, or belonged to, or more importantly why they'd left this little bundle of joy in *his* car.

His cop's instincts kicked in and he began looking for clues as to the baby's identity. The kid contraption had a faded yellow and white baby blanket tucked around it. Fearful of disturbing the baby, he gingerly picked up the corners of the blanket with two fingers, trying to see if there were any tags or identifying marks.

Nothing.

Carefully, hands shaking, he examined the child's clothing. The baby was dressed in a worn cloth diaper that was impeccably clean, and thankfully dry, but obviously not new. The faded yellow T-shirt the kid had on was also clean, but had obviously seen better days. There were no markings or identification of any kind on either.

One tiny white sock had been kicked off and now lay on the top of the front seat headrest, while the other sock remained on the kid's turbulent foot. A frayed pink bow made out of dime-store variety ribbon was neatly tied to a tuft of hair that grew out of the top of the kid's head like a wild mound of strawberry crabgrass.

No clues there. Except perhaps the kid needed a new barber.

He frowned at the baby, one large finger gently, reverently touching the pink bow. The fact that the ribbon was pink might lead him to believe the baby was a girl.

A baby girl.

In his car.

Abandoned.

Sweat broke out on his forehead, and for the first time in memory Danny Sullivan got scared.

Stumped, he stared at the baby, wondering what in the hell was going on? Why would someone leave a baby in his car? Danny shook his head. Didn't make sense.

Growing nervous, Danny stared at the baby much the way a man would stare at a mysterious ticking package. He didn't have much experience with babies. They were so little and so loud that they were the only things in the world that could scare the dickens out of him, probably because they made him feel totally...inept. Something a man with his confidence and his ego found totally and utterly appalling.

The only child he'd had any experience with was his little niece, Emma, his brother Michael's little girl. But Emma had just had her first birthday, and he didn't think bouncing her on his knee or giving her piggyback rides qualified him as much of a baby expert.

So why would someone leave a baby in *his* car?

Danny stared at the baby, and as if sensing his stare, she slowly turned to look at him. For a moment, Danny's heart seemed to slow as those beautiful eyes, so big, so blue, so incredibly...innocent and vulnerable honed in on him.

Danny swallowed.

Hard.

The little lady's eyes seemed to search his, watching, waiting expectantly, looking for something. Something all little kids deserved and were entitled to. Love. Security. Stability.

The baby waved one tiny, chubby fist in the air, then grabbed his finger trustingly, holding on as if her life depended on him.

In that instant, Danny realized it did....

SOMETIMES BIG SURPRISES COME IN SMALL PACKAGES!

Celebrate the happiness that only a baby can bring in Bundles of Joy by Silhouette Romance!

February 1998
On Baby Patrol by Sharon De Vita (SR#1276)
Bachelor cop Michael Sullivan pledged to protect his best friend's pregnant widow, Joanna Grace. Would his secret promise spark a vow to love, honor and cherish? Don't miss this exciting launch of Sharon's *Lullabies and Love* miniseries!

April 1998
Boot Scootin' Secret Baby by Natalie Patrick (SR#1289)
Cowboy Jacob Goodacre discovered his estranged wife, Alyssa, had secretly given birth to his daughter. Could a toddler with a fondness for her daddy's cowboy boots keep her parents' hearts roped together?

June 1998
Man, Wife and Little Wonder by Robin Nicholas (SR#1301)
Reformed bad boy Johnny Tremont would keep his orphaned niece at any price. But could a marriage in name only to pretty Grace Marie Green lead to the love of a lifetime?

And be sure to look for additional BUNDLES OF JOY titles
in the months to come.

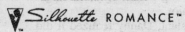

Find us at your favorite retail outlet.

Take 4 bestselling love stories FREE

a FREE surprise gift!

Special Limited-time Offer

Mail to Silhouette Reader Service™

3010 Walden Avenue
P.O. Box 1867
Buffalo, N.Y. 14240-1867

YES! Please send me 4 free Silhouette Romance™ novels and my free surprise gift. Then send me 6 brand-new novels every month, which I will receive months before they appear in bookstores. Bill me at the low price of $2.90 each plus 25¢ delivery and applicable sales tax, if any.* That's the complete price and a savings of over 10% off the cover prices—quite a bargain! I understand that accepting the books and gift places me under no obligation ever to buy any books. I can always return a shipment and cancel at any time. Even if I never buy another book from Silhouette, the 4 free books and the surprise gift are mine to keep forever.

215 SEN CF2P

Name	(PLEASE PRINT)	
Address		Apt. No.
City	State	Zip

**Make a Valentine's date
for the premiere of**

◆ HARLEQUIN® **Movies**

starting February 14, 1998 with

Debbie Macomber's

This Matter of

Marriage

on **the movie**  **channel** ⓣⓜⓒ

Just tune in to **The Movie Channel** the **second Saturday night** of every month at 9:00 p.m. EST to join us, and be swept away by the sheer thrill of romance brought to life. Watch for details of upcoming movies—in books, in your television viewing guide and in stores.

If you are not currently a subscriber to The Movie Channel, simply call your local cable or satellite provider for more details. Call today, and don't miss out on the romance!

the movie channel ⓣⓜⓒ
*100% pure movies.
100% pure fun.*

◆ HARLEQUIN™
™ *Makes any time special.*™

Harlequin is a trademark of Harlequin Enterprises Limited. The Movie Channel is a trademark of Showtime Networks, Inc., a Viacom Company.

An Alliance Production

HMBPA298

Return to the Towers!

In March
New York Times bestselling author

NORA ROBERTS

brings us to the Calhouns' fabulous
Maine coast mansion and reveals the
tragic secrets hidden there for generations.

For all his degrees, Professor Max Quartermain has a
lot to learn about love—and luscious Lilah Calhoun is
just the woman to teach him. Ex-cop Holt Bradford is
as prickly as a thornbush—until Suzanna Calhoun's
special touch makes love blossom in his heart.
And all of them are caught in the race to solve
the generations-old mystery of a priceless
lost necklace…and a timeless love.

Lilah and Suzanna
THE
Calhoun Women

A special 2-in-1 edition containing
FOR THE LOVE OF LILAH and
SUZANNA'S SURRENDER

Available at your favorite retail outlet.